'Mum said she hoped that at Park Wood (all) Girls' School I'd learn some poise. I wasn't looking forward to it. I was leaving all my Junior School friends. I had an awful uniform. But then I met Fleur, found out about sausage inspection and discovered how to squash the class bully *and* made a completely amazing stage debut at the end of term Revue. . .'

Mickey Young
First Year
Park Wood Girls' School

Also by Mary Hooper

Short Cut to Love
Making Waves
Lexie
Cassie
Janey's Diary
Janey's Summer
School Friends 2: Star

MARY HOOPER

School Friends 1

FIRST TERM

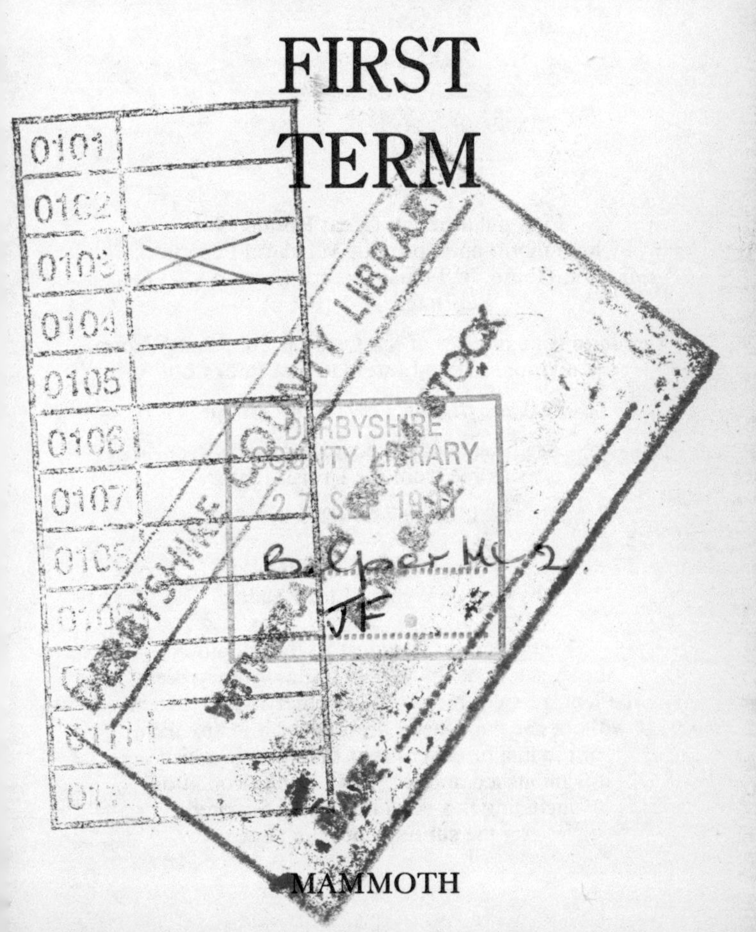

MAMMOTH

First published in Great Britain 1991
by Mammoth, an imprint of Mandarin Paperbacks
Michelin House, 81 Fulham Road, London SW3 6RB
Reprinted 1991 (twice)

Mandarin is an imprint of the Octopus Publishing Group,
a division of Reed International Books Ltd

A CIP catalogue record for this title
is available from the British Library

ISBN 0 7497 0295 8

Printed in Great Britain
by Cox & Wyman Ltd, Reading

Contents

One	'Do I *have* to?'	7
Two	Sausage inspection	23
Three	I reveal the dark secrets of the poison cupboard	33
Four	Annabel's swimming pool party	45
Five	Operation Alison	56
Six	Troubled waters	66
Seven	Crimewatch?	77
Eight	The facts of life	86
Nine	Sweet Home Economics!	97
Ten	'There's no business like Revue business. . .'	110

Chapter One

'DO I HAVE TO?'

I finished getting dressed and then stood by the window in the sitting-room, watching out for my friends to come by on their way to school. I stood well back and behind the curtain, though, so that they wouldn't see me when they did.

'All ready, Mickey?' Mum came up behind me and put a hand on my shoulder, making me jump. 'You look very nice in your uniform.'

I looked down at the bright red jumper, white blouse and navy skirt. 'I think I look revolting,' I said, pulling a face.

'Well, I think it looks very smart,' Mum said, putting the absolute kiss of death on it. 'And it's nice and cheerful-looking, as well.'

'It's the only thing that is, then,' I said gloomily.

'The first day's always the worst,' Mum said brightly. 'You'll be full of it by the time you get home, you wait and see.'

'Suppose I'm not; suppose I really hate it there, though?'

'Suppose you don't.'

'But suppose . . .' I saw a movement outside and leapt back from the window as if I'd been shot.

'Ouch!' Mum said, 'you got my foot again. You really must try and be a . . .'

'Get back!' I hissed at Mum, 'it's Carrie and Sally and everyone!'

'So what?' Mum said in surprise. 'You're still friends with them, aren't you? Just because you're going to a different school . . .'

I shushed her again and watched enviously as my old best friends went down the road towards school – towards the mixed comprehensive to which *I* would have been going but for Mum having some mad idea about wanting me to go to an all-girls school.

'No uniform, notice!' I said bitterly. 'And look how happy they look. They're not going to travel five miles on the bus – and probably feel sick – and then get put in a strange school with strange girls they've never seen before in their lives.'

'Just think how your character will be developed because of it, though,' Mum said in her best gushy and enthusiastic voice. 'Just think of all those wonderful opportunities to make friends with all sorts of different girls.'

I sighed. 'Millview was good enough for the boys, wasn't it? What's so different about me that I've got to go to a stupid single sex school?'

'It was different for your brothers. Anyway, Dad and I think a bit more female company would be good for you – following in Paul and Jamie's footsteps all the time is making you too much of a tomboy. I mean, you are a bit clumsy, aren't you? I hope that at Park Wood you may develop some poise.'

'Poise!' I said, and pulled an outraged face. I wasn't completely sure what it meant but it sounded twitty. 'Oh, so you want me in frilly dresses with bows in my hair and going to embroidery classes, do you?'

Mum laughed. 'You in a frilly dress I would like to see. Anyway, they don't have embroidery classes now – but you'll get equal opportunities in things like science and computing, whereas at Millview girls tend to get squashed out of those classes by the boys.'

'You sound just like the Park Wood brochure,' I said, and sighed again. 'I've got to go. The stupid bus arrives at the crossroads at eight-fifteen.' I looked at Mum darkly,'I just hope I'm not sick on it, that's all. You know I hate buses.'

'Just look straight ahead of you and you'll be perfectly all right,' Mum said. 'Now, where's your blazer?'

'Do I *have* to?'

'Of course you have to. It's part of the school uniform until it gets cold enough for the duffle coat.'

'Duffle coat!' I echoed in a doom-laden voice.

I picked up my school bag and slouched towards the door and Mum stood on the doorstep and beamed at me. 'You look lovely!' she said. 'It's the first time I've seen you look so neat and tidy since you were in your pram.'

I groaned. 'Do you mind? Someone might hear you.'

I looked up and down the road carefully before setting foot outside the gate. 'Go in!' I muttered to Mum. 'You're not going to stand there and wave me up the road, are you?'

'Not if you don't want me to,' Mum said, and she gave one last wave and went in but I saw her outlined against the opaque glass of the front door and knew she was still standing there ready to peer out.

Once round the corner I rolled my school skirt over and over at the waistband so it was shorter, pushed down the long white school socks and turned up the collar of my blazer so I didn't look quite as prissy and schoolgirlish. If I saw anyone I knew I'd put the school bag in front of my face and rush by, pretending not to see them. If I saw Carrie or any of that lot . . . but no, that didn't bear thinking about.

I hadn't exactly fallen out with all my old friends, but they just couldn't understand why I was going to Park Wood. I didn't blame them – I didn't, either. I'd told them all that I had had no say in where I went, that I couldn't help going to Park Wood, but they didn't want to know. They thought Mum and Dad must be snobs, sending me there – or that I was getting above myself.

I waited miserably on the corner for the bus, feeling a right twit in my uniform. Apart from screaming 'Park Wood!' at anyone who passed, it also screamed 'New Girl!', which was worse.

The school bus drew up and I tried to look old-girlish and casual.

'Park Wood?' I asked the driver politely.

He sighed. 'That's what it says on the front. We're not going to Harrods, are we?'

I climbed on and my bag slipped from my shoulder. Negotiating the stairs and hoping not to fall up them, I slung the bag a bit too enthusiastically back over my shoulder again and hit the girl in the first seat in the head. Great start . . .

I mumbled sorry and, falling over my feet, fell up the last step and looked round me, wondering where to sit. Towards the back of the bus sat some older girls, chattering and laughing together, but spaced out near the front were the obviously new first years with their glaringly new school uniforms and wary expressions. Should I sit next to one of them? Suppose she was waiting for a friend to get on, though? Suppose I sat next to someone who wouldn't speak to me? Why was everything so difficult?

'Do sit down, first year!' one of the bigger girls called from the back. 'The driver won't move until you do.'

'Oh! Sorry!' I said, in a panic at doing the wrong thing so early on, and quickly sat down on an empty seat opposite two dark-haired and dark-eyed first years. They were obviously twins because they looked exactly alike but one twin had her long hair in a bun on the top of her head and the other one had straight plaits right down her back. It was all right for them going to a new school – there were *two* of them.

I took a crafty look at the girl I'd slapped round the head with my duffle bag. She was definitely new because she still had a label sticking out of her blazer. She had lots of gold bangles sticking out of her blazer sleeve, beautifully cut bobbed hair and was wearing curved gold earrings with stones set along the edge. I stared at them; I'd read the school prospectus – Mum had shoved it in front of me often enough – and I knew that you were only allowed to wear small gold studs in your ears, certainly no glittering stones.

I couldn't see the girl who was sitting behind the driver very well, just that she was biggish, bigger than me (but then I'd been the almost-smallest in my last class) with curly hair pulled back off her face into an elastic band. She had her arms folded and looked solid and well-built.

There were two girls sitting together in front of me and I strained my ears to try and hear what they were saying. One had rather a silly, high voice and the other sounded older and more sensible. The sensible-sounding one had long, mousey-brown hair tucked behind her ears and a mousey-brown hair band holding it back.

'Well, I think we're really lucky to come to this school,' the squeaky voice said. 'Who wants to go where stupid boys are, anyway?'

'Actually, I didn't think of coming anywhere else,' the long-haired one said. 'My sister was here before me, you see. She was head girl.'

'Oh, fancy!' the other said, sounding impressed. 'I suppose you'll follow in her footsteps, then – be a prefect.'

'Oh, I don't know about that yet,' said the other one modestly.

The bus pulled up outside the school entrance and we climbed off. The older girls walked or ran off in different directions but we new ones just stood there pretending to be interested in a large tree in the grounds and wondering what to do next.

I'd seen the school before, of course. Mum had brought me to an open day and I'd also been for my interview with the head of lower school. Park Wood was an old house but it had had bits of newer buildings tacked on to it and there were a few portable flat-roofed buildings and sheds scattered around.

Just as I was wondering what we'd do if no one came for us – would we just stand lost in the playground for the rest of the day? – an older girl came out of the main doors. She was tall, with short fair hair and a big bust on which she wore a silver prefect's badge.

'Come along, Newies!' she said. 'Miss Green's waiting for you in the office.'

We obeyed her, picked up our bags and followed. Just as we reached the door a car pulled up behind us on the gravel driveway.

'Yoo hoo!' a woman's voice called. 'You're all new little first years, aren't you?' She didn't wait for a reply or realise that we were all glowering at her, outraged, but spoke to a girl in the car. 'There you are then, Cerise. Here's all your new friends!'

The girl emerged. She had frizzy blonde hair and a big pink lace bow stuck on the back of her head. She was wearing school uniform – sort of – but the red jumper was red, fluffy, soft stuff and the navy skirt was very short, and instead of being A-line it was tight. Underneath this trailed a pair of pale, knobbly legs and – most gasp-making of all –

white high-heeled boots.

'Hello,' she muttered to us, and her bottom lip quivered.

'Now, I'll just come in with you, shall I?' her mum said, 'and then I can see you all nicely settled.' She was wearing a black fluffy jumper which was embroidered all over with rhinestones or diamonds or something.

'Excuse me, you can't leave that car there.' The busty prefect had come out again. 'That's strictly school buses only and there'll be another one arriving any minute.'

'Oh, but I do want to see my Cerise well taken care of before I go home!' the woman said.

'Your Cerise will be well looked after, never fear,' the prefect said. 'You really needn't come in with her.'

'What d'you think, sweetheart?' the woman asked Cerise. 'Will you be all right on your own?'

Cerise's lower lip wobbled again and all at once the woman swept her into her arms. 'There, there,' she said, 'Mummy won't leave until you're sure!' And she pressed Cerise's face into the glittery stones.

'Yes, well, we'll just leave Cerise and her mother to it, shall we?' the prefect said, ushering us in and turning down my blazer collar at the same time. 'Maybe she'll make it indoors by Break.'

Giggling, we formed an untidy group in

the hallway and then followed her into the office.

'What did you think of that little show?' the girl with curved gold earrings asked me. 'Absolutely gross, don't you think?'

'Absolutely!' I agreed, feeling grateful that (a) she didn't seem to mind that I'd slapped her round the head and (b) I hadn't let Mum drive me to school.

Registration didn't take long. We just had to say who we were and have our details checked off on our record cards. I found out that the girl with gold earrings was called Annabel, the twins were Jasbir (plaits) and Arina (bun), the one whose sister had been head girl was Alice, next to her on the bus with the whiney voice had been Philippa, and Alison was the sturdy, rather hard-faced girl. As well as all these there was a big fat girl called Fleur, a black girl called Erica and someone I'd seen before – a Chinese girl called Su whose mum and dad ran the Takeaway in the next town.

When we were almost finished in Mrs Green's office, a red-faced and tearful Cerise came in, prodded through the door by a teacher.

'I found this one outside clinging to her mother,' the teacher said, 'I thought I'd better rescue her.'

'Ah, Mrs Mackie,' Mrs Green said, 'I was just about to send for you. Most of these first years are yours, you can take them along to their classroom if you like.'

Mrs Mackie rolled her eyes and pointed at Cerise over the top of her head. 'This one as well, I suppose?' she said in a weary voice, and Mrs Green laughed.

I looked carefully at Mrs Mackie; I'd already been told that she was my teacher but I hadn't seen her before. She was fiftyish, I suppose, with smooth grey hair pulled back off her face, old-fashioned glasses and a shrewd, rather sharp expression. She looked a bit strict. I realised at once it would be extremely difficult to pull the wool over *her* eyes.

She walked towards the door and, because she was burdened down with files and a register, I suddenly thought what a wonderful impression it would make if I opened the door for her. The trouble was, I pulled it open a little too quickly and a little too enthusiastically and somehow the side of the door hit the files and they all went up in the air, making papers flutter in the air all around.

'Sorry!' I said, as about six of us bobbed down to pick them up and all bumped heads.

'Thank you! Those are confidential papers – I'll pick them up myself,' Mrs Mackie said. She stooped down and looked at me over her glasses, 'And what's your name?'

'Mickey. Michelle Young,' I said, and gave her a sickly smile.

A crowd of us followed her along the corridors to her classroom, where another little group of first years were waiting. Mrs Mackie taught history so our form room was in fact the History Room for the whole school. The walls were decorated with posters showing kings and queens of England and the different dynasties. One wall housed the lockers where we could keep our things.

While we looked around us and were allocated our lockers, Mrs Mackie started telling us some school rules, especially what we had to do at lunch times. Apparently we weren't allowed to stay in class unless there was a hurricane or snow up to the windows or something.

'But even then there must be no eating in classrooms, and no going out of the school.' She looked round at us severely, 'You are only allowed out if you're going home for lunch and I don't suppose many of you are because of the distances involved.'

'I am,' Cerise said. 'Mummy said she'd come and take me home for the first month or so, just until I get settled.'

'Yes, I thought she might,' Mrs Mackie said dryly. 'Now, if you'd all like to choose a desk and may I have short-sighted girls at the front, please.'

Well, I don't quite know how it happened but I'd been lounging against the wall listening to her going on and somehow, as I'd lounged, a piece of poster had stuck itself to me so that when I moved away to bag a seat the poster came too, curling off the wall with a sickly tearing sound.

'Oh, really! Do take care,' Mrs Mackie said as I fought to get out of its clutches, and then she frowned. 'That's you again is it? Michelle Young?'

'Yes,' I said weakly.

By the time I'd climbed out of the poster and re-stuck it to the wall in three pieces, most of the good seats had gone and I found myself next to Philippa, which didn't exactly thrill me: she had a nasty weasely little face and a funny crafty smile.

'Now, let's go through a few basic school rules,' Mrs Mackie said, 'and the first of these is uniform. Stand up, Cerise, please.'

Cerise stood up, sniffed and looked around her. She wiped her nose on the back of her fluffy jumper.

'As you can see, Cerise is not wearing school uniform,' Mrs Mackie said.

'It's the right colours,' Cerise said indignantly.

'The colours are right, but I'm afraid that's all. Just so we know, can any one tell me what's wrong with Cerise's outfit?'

Alice put her hand up. 'It's not a regulation jumper,' she said, 'and the skirt should be an A-line skirt. Also she should have proper school shoes – not boots with heels.'

'Well, the proper red jumper was all scratchy and horrid and Mummy said the A-line skirt wasn't flattering to a young figure,' Cerise said. 'We thought this would be all right.'

'I see,' Mrs Mackie said. 'Well, I'm afraid scratchy or unflattering or not, the proper, regulation uniform must be worn. Perhaps your mother could take you out at lunchtime and buy you one.'

'Oh, but we were going to McDonalds for a . . .'

Mrs Mackie turned a steely eye on Cerise and she shut up abruptly. 'And no bows in the hair, either, Cerise. And while we're on the subject of hair, the headmistress says that if it reaches the shoulders, it must be tied back.'

I twiddled with my own, pulling it straight. It just about reached my shoulders if I pulled at it, but not if I kept my head moving about. I hate having it scraped away from my face; I look like a spaniel when you pull its ears back. Besides, I like to be able to fiddle with it and nibble the ends occasionally.

'Earrings.' Mrs Mackie said. 'You've all read our brochure – earrings have to be studs only; any others will be confiscated.' She looked across at Annabel and went on, 'As will any jewellery whatsoever, apart from a very plain watch marked with your name.'

Annabel jangled her array of gold bangles. 'I suppose that means me,' she said, reaching up to unclip her earrings. She handed everything including her watch to Mrs Mackie. 'I'll get them back after school, will I?' she said. 'They're worth quite a lot of money, you see.'

'Well then, how very foolish to wear them here,' Mrs Mackie said crisply, but Annabel just shrugged and sat down.

We were taken through the rest of the school rules and then Mrs Mackie said she wanted to ask for our help.

'During the Christmas term, each form adopts a charity,' she said, 'and there's always a certain amount of rivalry between forms as to who can raise the most money and win the silver shield which the headmistress presents. Last year . . .' she smiled warmly at the memory, 'my own first-formers who are now second formers, of course, won the shield. Of course, I can't expect you to do as well as they did, but I would like you all to pull together and make a big effort.

'You may choose your own charity and are encouraged to devise your own ways of earning money. Some forms hold jumble sales, some sell Christmas cards, some run sponsored walks – it'll be up to you to decide between you what you're good at and what will earn the most money. Just do your best for me.'

Annabel put her hand up. 'Can't we just bring money in from our parents?' she said, 'it would be so much easier.'

Mrs Mackie looked at her beadily. 'That is not the idea, Annabel,' she said. 'Not all our families can afford it, and the whole idea is that we all pull together and work as a team. If people were to start bringing money in from home it would defeat the whole object of the exercise.'

'Oh,' Annabel said.

'Bet she's really rich,' Philippa said next to me in a low voice. 'Bet she's absolutely rolling in it. I mean, just look at her clothes.'

I leaned sideways out of my seat, all the better to look at Annabel in her 'Designer' school uniform. Philippa was right – her shoes were really soft leather and her . . .

'Michelle Young! Are you with us?' Mrs Mackie barked. 'What is so interesting about Annabel's feet?'

'Nothing, Mrs Mackie,' I said, going as red as my jumper, and sitting upright and scraping my chair back with what came out as a noisy squeal.

Mrs Mackie put her hands over her ears. 'I did hope for some quiet, well-behaved girls this year . . .' She looked at me and shook her head. 'Perhaps that's too much to expect . . .'

Chapter Two
SAUSAGE INSPECTION

I reached the service counter in the dining hall, balanced a glass of water on my tray and wondered whether or not to take a fizzy drink as well. Or a milk shake. Or fruit juice. I dawdled thoughtfully . . . I'd never had so much choice before. At primary school we'd just got our meals slopped in front of us, like them or lump them. Usually lump them. This, though, was different, there were actual choices: sausages, salads, sandwiches, chicken . . . I hesitated, my hand hovering first over the sausages, then the cornish pasties, then the flan.

'Get a move on!' an older, blonde girl behind me said crossly. 'Some of us have got lunchtime clubs to go to.'

'Sorry!' I said quickly, and my hand darted

out and picked up a cornish pasty.

'Use the tongs!' the red-faced girl behind her commanded. 'What d'you think they're there for?'

I shot her an anguished smile and, obediently picking up the tongs, removed the cornish pasty from my plate and put it back on the shelf, then moved it back to my plate again. All without dropping it – I was really quite pleased with myself.

'I don't believe it,' the blonde one groaned.

'Have you quite finished?' red face said.

'Well, I haven't, quite . . .' I was starving and Mum had said that, as it was my first day, I could have as much as I wanted to eat. I moved three cold sausages on to my plate, all with the tongs. One slipped out halfway across and dropped into a bowl of salad but I got it out quite easily.

'Playing shops?' the red-faced one asked sarcastically.

'Sorry,' I muttered, and then I quickly took a couple of tomatoes and a slice of bread.

'First day?' red face asked, and I nodded.

They exchanged glances. 'Don't forget to report to the head girl, then,' the blonde one said.

I stopped with a bowl of fruit salad halfway to my tray. 'What for?'

'Oh, it's a school custom. All new girls at lunch time on their first day have to go and see Karen Kemp.'

I sighed. Another ordeal to face.

'She says a few words to all new girls about . . .'

'About their lunch,' red face put in quickly. 'She inspects it. You have to go up to her with your food and say, 'Hello Karen, I've come for sausage inspection . . .'

I looked at her in amazement. 'Hello Karen I've come for sausage inspection?'

'That's right.' The blonde one put down her tray. 'That's her up there, on the top table with the prefects. She's got her hair up and a badge saying Head Girl. Just go straight up – she'll be expecting you.'

I sighed again. 'All right . . .'

'Everyone does,' red face assured me. 'She gets really angry if you don't.'

I paid for everything on my tray – I only just had enough money – and, balancing it all carefully, walked down the hall. It was about three times as big as the dining hall in primary school and about ten times as noisy. I was dead scared I'd drop something but the practising I'd been doing at home ready for this – walking up and down with mum's best tea set laid out on a wooden tray – must have helped. In view of my track record I needed as many tips as I could get and Mum had given me another tip and that was to hum 'Here Comes the Bride' quietly under my breath. Apparently it made you walk straight and keep everything steady. It was only when I'd almost reached Karen's table that I realised everyone was looking at me strangely, so I must have been humming it too loudly. I stopped just before I approached her table because someone else was standing beside her – another new girl going up for her few words of wisdom, perhaps – and looked down at my tray. It was very crowded . . . I bet she'd think I was really greedy. I maybe shouldn't have had all those sausages . . .

Cleverly balancing the tray in one hand for a split second, I whipped off a sausage and stuffed it into my pocket. I could get it out later.

I approached the table humbly and coughed to get her attention. 'Karen?' I asked. (Should it be Miss Kemp, perhaps?) 'I'm new today . . . I was told I had to come and see you.'

'What for?' she asked, frowning.

'So you could . . . er . . . look at my lunch.' I realised for the first time how dippy it sounded. 'For . . . er . . . sausage inspection,' I added lamely.

She looked at me and burst out laughing and so did the rest of her table.

'Who told you that?'

I smiled a sickly smile. 'Two girls in the queue.'

'Well, I'm afraid you've been had!' she said.

I started backing away, my face as red as my jumper, my tray wobbling dangerously. Any second I expected to slip over, throw the tray over my head and fill the air with flying cornish pasty. How could I have believed them? Why on earth hadn't I realised they were having me on?

'Sorry!' I called, walking backwards as fast as I could. 'Sorry to have bothered you!'

'That's all right,' she called back above the noise. 'You gave us a laugh.'

I took the long route down the hall to give my face time to stop being red and found Alison, the twins and Fleur sitting near the door.

'Over here – there's a space!' Alison said bossily, and though I'd already decided I didn't much like her, I went over anyway just for the sake of being with someone I knew.

'Where have you been?' Fleur asked. 'I saw you in the queue ages ago.'

I settled myself down and placed all my food around me carefully. 'I went to see Karen Kemp. She's the head girl, you know.'

'What d'you go and see her for?' Arina asked.

'Oh, you have to,' I said, hoping I wasn't going red again, 'it's a school custom on your first day. You go up and see her and she . . . inspects your lunch.'

Everyone burst out laughing. Jasbir got up in a great hurry. 'Oh, I'd better go and see her now!' she said. 'No one told me about that and I've already eaten my lunch and she hasn't inspected it!'

Arina grabbed her. 'Daft!' she said. 'Mickey's having us on. It's a joke, isn't it, Mickey?'

I smiled brightly. 'Course!' I said.

Jasbir sat down again. 'Thought it was,' she said.

'No, you didn't!' Arina said. 'You would have gone right up there if I'd let you.'

'Course I wouldn't! How stupid d'you think I am?'

'Very stupid indeed! You always . . .'

I turned away from the twins who'd been arguing like that all morning and asked Fleur what she was going to do for the Charity Shield.

'Don't know,' she shrugged. 'I'm not much good at making things to sell.'

I shook my head. 'Neither am I. I made a cushion cover in my last school and I forgot to leave an opening to put the cushion in.'

'*I'm* good at making things,' Alison said. 'I made beautiful Christmas cards last year out of old milk bottle tops.'

'We could do something sponsored,' Philippa said – she and Annabel had joined us – 'a sponsored walk or litter pick up or something.'

'But they're so boring!' Annabel said.

'How about a sponsored swim, then?' Fleur suggested.

Philippa shuddered. 'I hate swimming! It's always so cold and smelly!'

'Well, you could come to my house and do it,' Annabel said, 'our swimming pool's not cold.'

We all looked at her. 'You've got a swimming pool *inside*?' I asked, and she nodded.

'Could we really all use it, though?' Fleur asked. 'The whole class?'

'I think so,' Annabel said, not quite so readily. 'Well, my dad's always complaining that it's not used enough.'

'We could get people to sponsor us for a certain amount per length,' Philippa said, and she looked up into Annabel's face with a silly, fawning expression. 'Fancy having a swimming pool inside! I bet your house is really huge, isn't it? Have you got a sauna as well. I love saunas . . .'

'We can't *just* have a sponsored swim,' I interrupted quickly, trying to stop Philippa's grovels. 'It wouldn't be enough. We want to make lots of money.' I searched my mind wildly for ideas and was suddenly struck by one. 'As well as the sponsored swim we could have a pantomime! Invite all our relatives.'

'What sort of a pantomime?' Fleur asked.

'In your case – Billy Bunter!' Alison said nastily, but no one laughed.

'I hate pantomimes,' Annabel said. 'They're so corny. And they're for babies – all that shouting, "He's behind you!" and all that.'

'*I* hate them, too,' Philippa said quickly.

'It need not be a proper traditional pantomime,' I said. 'It could be like a revue.'

'What's that?' Fleur asked.

'Well, it's bits and pieces of all sorts of

things: funny sketches, people singing and dancing and telling jokes and all that.'

'Sounds all right,' Fleur said.

Everyone had finished so we got up and went outside just in time to see Cerise coming across the playground wearing her new uniform.

'Mummy was furious she had to buy more things!' she reported. 'And see how awful this uniform looks on me. Red makes me look so washed out.'

'You will be washed out if Mrs Mackie sees you've still got that bow in your hair,' Annabel said.

Cerise patted her mop of frizz and pouted. 'But I always like to wear something cerise because of my name,' she said. 'Just a little touch of pink somewhere . . .'

Several of us giggled. 'Perhaps you should tell Mrs Mackie that,' I said, trying to keep a straight face.

'And I think I should be allowed to wear a flower in my hair because my name's Fleur!' Fleur said.

Cerise thought we meant it. 'D'you think I should mention it to Mrs Mackie?' she asked, and we all nodded solemnly.

She didn't ask, though, because when we went in for afternoon register Mrs Mackie seemed to be in a bit of a bad mood, which wasn't helped by me getting an instant sneeze during her calling of the register and, on diving into my pocket for a hanky, pulling out a sausage.

It rolled gently towards the front of the class and she looked over towards it and then did a double-take, as if she couldn't quite believe her eyes. Well, I suppose it's not often you see a pork sausage moving slowly down the classroom.

'What is this?' she asked.

I put up my hand. 'A pork sausage,' I said. Well, it was, wasn't it?

'Oh dear, oh dear, oh dear . . .' was all she said.

On the way home on the bus that afternoon I got out my new rough book and made a list of the girls I'd got to know, giving them a rating as possible best friends.

Alison	– *too big and bossy*
Annabel	– *possible. Bit too posh?*
Cerise	– *certainly not*
Arina &	– *won't want to be best friends*
Jasbir	– *because they've got each other*
Alice	– *too goody–goody*
Philippa	– *yuk. Anyway, she's all over Annabel*
Fleur	– *possible. If not so fat.*

I looked at the list and thought about my ex-best friend, wondering how she'd got on on her first day. She'd promised to ring me to tell me, but I knew she wouldn't: she'd promised to ring me too many other days for me to believe that. Whilst thinking about Carrie and that lot, though, I forgot what I was doing and let my rough book and all my homework books slip off my lap and onto the floor. I just hoped that Alison, who was sitting the other side of the aisle to me, couldn't read upside down . . .

Chapter Three

I REVEAL THE DARK SECRETS OF THE POISON CUPBOARD

'D'you mind Alison having goes at you all the time?' I asked Fleur curiously. It was a couple of weeks into term and we were waiting outside the science lab one morning ready to go in for a double lesson.

She shook her head and shrugged. 'When you're fat, someone always *does* have goes,' she said. 'And I am fat, aren't I?'

I looked at her cautiously. She was certainly a bit of a porker, but it seemed a bit off to say so.

'Go on, you can say it,' she said. 'I'm used to it.'

'Don't you mind?'

'I've always been big. When I was a baby they had to reinforce my pram with steel girders.'

I giggled. 'Really?'

'No, not really,' she said. It's just the sort of thing you have to say when you're fat – and you have to say it before they do.'

'I don't much like her, do you?' I said in a low voice, looking round to make sure Alison wasn't standing behind me ready to twist my arm behind my back or dig me in the side with her ever-ready elbow.

'Alison? She's a toad,' Fleur said. 'And she's a thief. I saw her get a 'Kit-Kat' off Philippa yesterday and on Monday she took a can of drink off Jasbir.'

'I know,' I said indignantly, 'and she had a 'Bounty' off me last week! What can we do, though?'

'Not a lot.' Fleur said. 'She's bigger than us.' She laughed, 'well, maybe not bigger than *me*, just stronger and bullier.'

Mrs Evans, the science teacher, came bustling along and smiled at us as she opened the lab door. 'You lot are keen, aren't you?' she said, 'I expect you'll get over it by the second year.'

Mrs Evans was nice, a big woman with short brown hair and long droopy skirts that fell around her ankles. I liked her and I liked science, although we hadn't actually done anything very scientific yet, just played with litmus papers and made up temperature charts. I liked the nice, smelly atmosphere in there, though, and the jars of strange-coloured things and the intriguing cupboard at the back of the room labelled Poison Cupboard. Mrs Evans had told us that she kept the key to the cupboard round her neck and never took it off, not even in bed.

That day I was quite relieved to see how friendly she was towards me, because the week before I'd got into a spot of trouble with some mercury: mine had escaped from its little beaker and rolled along the bench to smash into a million pieces on the floor. I'd managed to collect it nicely into one globule again, but quite a lot of floor stuff had gone into the beaker too, and she hadn't been very pleased.

We formed twos, found places behind the benches and she started us off on an experiment to make soap. One of the student teachers came in and she and Mrs Evans started going over our next week's work. While they were busily chatting and all of us lot – Erica was my partner – were trying to squish together something that looked nothing at all like soap, Philippa piped up behind us:

'Of course, you know what's in that poison cupboard, don't you?'

'Poison?' Erica suggested.

'No. Bits of bodies!'

We all stopped squishing and looked round.

'Don't be utterly stupid,' Alison said. 'Would the school really be allowed to have bits of bodies in there?'

'There's things that have been removed from people,' Philippa went on in her know-all voice. 'Arms and hearts and kidneys and all those sorts of things. They're in this special stuff that pickles them forever and you can take them out and look at them.'

'Who'd want to look at them?' I said with a shudder.

'Girls who're interested in being nurses and doctors, I'spose,' Philippa said. 'Anyway, it's true. If you're in the top stream in your final year you're allowed to take them out of the jars and handle them.'

'I don't believe you!' Fleur said.

'It's true! Honestly it is! And that's not all,' she added in a low voice, 'there's something else even more interesting.'

We all forgot about the soap completely.

'There's a man's you-know – *thingy*! In a jar!'

'There's not!' Cerise said with a startled shriek, and we all started giggling and nudging each other – all of us except for Alice, that is. She was always practising to be head girl; I suppose she felt she had to keep up with her sister.

'Don't be so ridiculous,' she said, turning away as if she wanted nothing more to do with us. 'Elizabeth came to this school and she never told me anything about things in jars.'

'Perhaps she wasn't in the top science class,' Philippa said.

'She was head girl!' Alice said witheringly, 'she was in the top everything.'

'Maybe she's so frightfully polite she didn't like to mention it,' Alison said.

'Girls!' Mrs Evans said mildly, 'what's all the noise? What's so terribly interesting that you have to leave your experiments?'

'Nothing,' we all murmured, going back to the squishing.

'D'you think it's true?' I asked Erica.

She shrugged. 'Dunno. Philippa loves to have a bit of gossip to spread, doesn't she? I reckon she's just making it up.'

I nodded. 'All the better to get Annabel's attention,' I said. 'Isn't it sick the way she fawns all over her?'

'Pathetic!' Erica agreed. She had a shock of frizzy black hair and she pushed it back out of her eyes as she spoke: *'Oh Annabel you do look nice today; Oh, Annabel your house sounds so lovely; Oh Annabel do let me lie on the floor so you can use me as a doormat,'* she whined in a high-pitched and perfect imitation of Philippa.

I burst into giggles. 'That was great! It sounded exactly like her! I bet you could do something on stage for the Revue, couldn't you?'

'If you like,' Erica said, pleased. 'I can do all sorts of people – I keep my little sisters amused by doing *Eastenders*. I could do some of the teachers, too.'

'Go on, then,' I urged her.

She cleared her throat and her face slipped into a bland mask, *'Girls, I really shouldn't have to remind you to stand up when the headmistress comes into the room,'* she said in a perfect Mrs Mackie, *'Of course, I never had to remind my last year's first years, but there you are. I'm afraid things are sadly altered now.'*

I clapped my hands. 'Brilliant!'

Mrs Evans, long black dress trailing round her ankles, glided up towards the back of the class where we were standing behind the lab benches. 'All right, girls?' she asked pleasantly.

'Yes, Mrs Evans!' we chorused.

'I'm just going to pop along to the secretary's office with the student teacher for a moment. You'll keep order, won't you, Alice?' she asked, and Alice nodded proudly as Mrs Evans swished out.

As soon as they'd gone Philippa started up again about the gruesome things to be found in the poison cupboard. The less notice we took of her the more outrageous her stories got until it seemed that Mrs Evans had collected enough spare parts to have at least three Frankenstein's monsters lying in there all sewn up and ready to go.

'Go on! I don't believe a word of it!' I said to Philippa. 'It's just a joke, isn't it? Mrs Evans wouldn't be allowed to have bit of bodies everywhere. They'd smell!'

'I told you – they're all in preserving fluid so they can't go off,' she said. 'Anyway, I know people who've actually seen them.'

'Go on!'

'It's true!' Philippa said, squeakily indignant. 'Why don't you believe me – I know lots of things you don't!'

I glanced to the back wall and the poison cupboard. Mrs Evans had gone in there earlier to get something for our experiment and I wondered if possibly . . .

'Don't leave the bench please, Mickey,' Alice said in an important voice.

'Just thought I'd see . . .' I said, and my voice trailed off as I reached the poison cupboard and turned the handle. The door opened!

'You wouldn't dare!' I heard Alison say behind me, and before I knew what I was doing I'd pushed open the door and gone in.

'Come out at once!' Alice said, but I scarcely heard her because I was inside and looking hurriedly around the shelves. There were no windows so it was very dark, of course, and as I didn't dare to put on the light I left the door ajar slightly so I could see.

My heart beating very fast, I looked round, hardly hearing the murmur of excited voices outside. Now, where would spare parts of people be kept? Philippa had said big jars, but there didn't appear to be any. There were all sorts of other interesting things, though: coloured bottles of strange liquids, packets of things with funny names, wicker baskets stuffed with papers, shiny wooden boxes with locks, a glass cabinet filled with little bottles.

My eyes searched frantically along the shelves: there were no spare parts of people, definitely not – not unless they were inside those large unmarked cardboard cartons on the top shelf . . . There was a stepladder propped up against one wall and I made a grab for it – and just at that moment heard the smooth voice of Mrs Evans outside asking, 'Everything all right, Alice?'

I heard the rest of the girls murmur something and then Mrs Evans said, 'You seem to be working well, girls. Keep it up,' and then: 'Good heavens, I've left the poison cupboard open!'

I held my breath as her footsteps came towards the cupboard. I should have spoken up there and then, I suppose, owned up that I was inside, but I just couldn't, not now I was actually inside the forbidden place.

I held my breath; there was the sound of a key turning in the lock, then a click, then Mrs Evans' muffled footsteps walking away. I pictured the faces of the others outside, and nearly giggled, and then I thought of myself, inside, and stopped. It was pitch dark now and I was trapped. Suppose there wasn't enough air in here? Suppose no one said I was in here because they didn't want to sneak, so I suffocated? Suppose – well, it was awfully dark and scarey – all the spare parts of people got together and leapt on me?

My hands tightened on the stepladder . . . I'd have to use that to fight them off with – that's if I hadn't already fainted from lack of air.

Now my eyes were getting used to the dark, though, I could see that some light was getting in from a ventilation brick near the top. And air, too, of course, so I wouldn't suffocate. Maybe there was just enough light to get up and look at those cardboard cartons on the top shelf . . .

Quiet as a mouse, I pulled the stepladder into position under the shelf and began to climb up. I couldn't hear anything from outside now. Presumably everyone else was writing up their notes and, Mrs Evans hadn't noticed I'd disappeared.

I climbed to the top of the ladder and carefully – very carefully, I didn't want to be covered in spare arms and legs – I reached out for one of the cartons, pulled it to me and, clutching it to my chest, climbed down with it.

My fingers were trembling as I pulled open the top and pulled out a big heavy jar containing a dim, yellowy fluid – preserving fluid? – and also containing a large floating something-or-other. I felt round the jar for a label and at last found one on the bottom: *Diseased human liver* it said, and I nearly dropped the bottle in my excitement.

She'd been right! Much as I hated to say it, she'd been telling the truth; the other bottles probably contained other more interesting bits. Of course, I had to find out what, now that I was actually in there. I replaced the liver bottle and brought down another one: *human appendix* and the third and last contained - *lung tissue*!

I climbed back up with the lung tissue. Philippa had been right, but not all that right. I mean, there'd been nothing *really* interesting.

And now all I had to do was get out . . .

There was a great skidding around of chairs from outside – the lesson was over and everyone was clearing up. Silently I put back the stepladder and stood by the door, wondering what to do. Could I start knocking to come out, perhaps, and then pretend to Mrs Evans that I'd gone in, fainted, and just woken up? Should I stay there until the cleaners came and get one of them to let me out? Should I say something had fallen on my head and made me lose my memory? What if Mrs Evans went really mad and reported me to the head, though?

There was a noise from outside and then the sound of a key turning in the lock. I froze against the wall; I hadn't yet decided what my story was going to be . . .

'I'll put the oil back on the shelf, shall I, Mrs

Evans?' Alice said in her best goody-goody voice, coming in carrying two bottles.

I blinked at the daylight suddenly coming in and gaped at Alice.

'Yes, thank you, Alice,' I heard Mrs Evans say.

'Crawl out and be quick about it!' Alice whispered, and I immediately dropped on all fours and, keeping as close to the ground as possible, crept away and back to my place.

'Anything else, Mrs Evans?' Alice – good old Alice – trilled, and Mrs Evans said no and thanked her for being so helpful. I was midway between the second and third benches by this time, still on all fours, and Fleur was patting me on the head like a dog as I passed.

I reached my space next to Erica and stood up, a bit red in the face. I started looking through her soap-squishing calculations.

'Most interesting,' I said to Erica. 'What did you think of that experiment? Of course, the manufacturers add a lot of other bits and pieces when they're making soap in bulk, don't they?'

'Never mind the soap,' she said in an undertone, 'what about the bodies?'

'Liver, appendix and lung,' I said breathlessly. 'No naughty bits.'

We both started giggling and Mrs Evans looked over at us, then at me in particular, slightly puzzled. 'You've certainly been nice and quiet this lesson, Michelle,' she said, 'no loud chatter, no accidents with mercury – why, I've hardly noticed that you've been here.' She gave a cheerful smile, 'Keep it up, dear.'

Chapter Four

ANNABEL'S SWIMMING POOL PARTY

We were on our way to Annabel's house, all jolly in the back of the school bus and singing 'We're all going to an indoor swimming pool!' Well, we weren't *all* jolly – Alison was just about as jolly as she ever got, which wasn't *very*, and Annabel was a bit quiet. Actually, she seemed to have changed her mind about having us all there. I think she'd only said we could come on an impulse, but with Philippa around there was no hopes of getting out of it. Every day she'd say, 'When are we coming to swim, then?' or 'Ooh, Annabel, I'm dying to see your pool!' and Alison would mutter nastily in the background: 'Bet she hasn't really got one,' until Annabel just had to invite us.

About ten of us had turned up. Some of the

class had things to do after school and some – the twins, for instance – hadn't been allowed to come. Arina had told me that her dad was dead strict on what they did after school; they were only allowed to go to places like the library. She said the only rebellion she'd got away with so far was being allowed to have her hair up. Her dad thought that both twins ought to have plaits, but she had managed to persuade him to be really daring and let her have her bun.

Annabel lived some way out and, when most of the others on the bus had been dropped off, we started talking about the Revue. We'd avoided the subject until now in case girls on the bus from other classes copied our idea.

It was quite sickening the way everyone seemed to be able to do something clever for it, everyone except me, that is. Alice was going to do a violin solo, Arina and Jasbir said they could do a traditional Pakistani dance and Cerise was going to do what she called a speciality number. This meant she'd be dressed as a cancan dancer and there would be lots of swooshing up of petticoats to show her knickers and a song all in broken English with plenty of 'Ooh-la-las'. Donna had said she was terrifically good at conjuring tricks, and Annabel went to tap dancing lessons and said she could probably do a short number. Philippa, on hearing this, said she was going to go to tap dancing lessons, too, and wouldn't it be gorgeous if they could do a double act?

We all waited for Annabel to explode, but she didn't say a thing. It was strange how she didn't seem to mind Philippa toadying and saying how wonderful she was all the time.

'What will you do then, Mickey?' Cerise asked. She was sitting next to me on the bus and smelt of hairspray, hair mousse, talc and cologne. Four different perfumes, naturally. She also had electric-blue mascara and little stick-on pink hearts on her ears instead of earrings.

'I don't know . . .' I said thoughtfully. I'd been worrying about it for some time; I'd been the one to think of doing the Revue, and I didn't have anything clever to do.

'I suppose I could get one of my brothers to teach me the guitar very quickly . . .'

'Brothers?' Cerise asked. 'I didn't know you had brothers. How many?'

'Three,' I said. 'One married, two still at home.'

'Ooh, you are lucky,' she said. 'Mummy says it's lovely to have brothers . . . she had two and they always brought lots of friends home so that when she was a teenager she was never short of a date.'

I pulled a face. I couldn't quite see that happening – none of their friends ever even spoke to me.

'Have they got nice friends?' she persisted. 'Is there anyone you specially like?'

'No, there isn't,' I said. 'They don't talk to me and I don't talk to them. Jamie and Paul are in a group now and . . .'

'A group!' she interrupted. 'Are they famous?'

'Not at all,' I said. 'Not the slightest bit.'

'How old are they? Are they good-looking?'

'One's fifteen and one's seventeen and no, they're not.'

'Sisters always say that, but I bet they are. Fancy having brothers who're in a group . . .' and her voice drifted away dreamily.

The bus stopped at the nearest point to Annabel's house and we got off and began straggling up a hill with Philippa dancing around Annabel all the way and saying what a lovely road it was.

We turned a corner, crossed a road, went through huge great wrought-iron gates and there we were, at Annabel's house. It was about six times as big as a normal house and set in a garden which looked more like a park. It was a modern house, though, and I'd been expecting an old manor house, something like they used in adverts for expensive cars.

We all trooped round the back where there was a huge conservatory thing with a swimming pool inside. It was lovely: lots of greenery hanging from the ceiling and statues and even a little row of changing rooms like the ones you get on the beach.

Annabel went off to see if there was anyone around, and apparently there wasn't because she told us all to get changed and get in the pool whenever we wanted.

I shared a changing room with Fleur and we were really excited, laughing and shrieking and throwing things about, but then when I was ready and about to go outside she just turned to me and said in a matter-of-fact voice, 'Oh, I've forgotten my swimsuit.'

I stared at her. 'I thought I saw it wrapped in your towel.'

She shook her head. 'It was my . . . my leotard. They're both black and I brought the wrong one.'

'But . . . but you were really looking forward to swimming. You said you were good at it.'

'Mmm,' she said, 'but never mind.'

'Perhaps Annabel's got a spare swimsuit. She's bound to have. They probably keep hundreds of them for visitors. Gold ones,' I giggled.

She didn't laugh. 'Oh yes, I'd fit into Annabel's swimsuit all right, wouldn't I?'

'Well, her mum might have one. She might be . . .' She might be fat, I'd been about to say.

'Well, she won't be as fat as me, that's for sure!' Fleur said in a jolly voice.

'What'll you do, then?'

'Sit around and watch you lot,' she said.

'D'you want me to ask if there's a spare one anywhere?'

'No,' she said. She caught my arm as I turned to go out, 'And Mickey . . . don't tell the others you thought you saw my swimsuit, will you?'

I shook my head. 'No, of course not.' So it hadn't really been her leotard . . .

When I opened the door, everyone else was out and changed and half of them were already in the pool. Fleur sat herself down on one of the wickerwork chairs at the deep end and said she'd time anyone who wanted to do lengths. No one did any timed lengths, though, we hardly remembered we were supposed to be planning a sponsored swim. It was just so nice to drift around in the warm water and pretend you were on holiday somewhere exotic.

I suppose we'd been there about half an hour, and I'd just climbed on a small board at the end to see if I could do a dive, when a tall woman in a white slinky dress and a lot of puffed up and very blonde hair appeared in the doorway, stopped dead and stared at us in absolute horror.

'Annabel!' she suddenly shouted above the din we were making. 'What on earth is going on?'

We all stopped splashing or swimming or whatever and absolute silence fell. Annabel swam to the side.

'H . . hello, Mum,' she said, and she'd gone bright red. 'It's just my friends from school.'

'So I see.' Her mum looked at us all and then spoke as if she had a dirty smell under her nose. 'I do wish you'd have asked first, Annabel.'

'Yes, well . . . you weren't here last night.'

'It's really not at all convenient. I've got the Peterson-Browns and the Gilberts coming over for supper and a swim. You don't think of these things, do you? It just doesn't occur to you that it might inconvenience me.'

We all stood stock still and embarrassed; Fleur looked as if she'd like to disappear into the wickerwork chair.

'No, well, I . . .' Annabel began.

'Oh, Mrs le Bon! Philippa interrupted, 'it's just that Annabel very kindly said we could come and try out the pool – for the sponsored swim, you know . . .'

Her voice died away at the look of horror on Annabel's mum's face.

'Sponsored swim?!' she said in the sort of tone she might have said sponsored rat hunt. 'There's certainly not going to be any sponsored swim in my pool! A bunch of schoolchildren cavorting about – certainly not!'

I don't quite know what happened then except I was cold and shivering a bit and, in rubbing my arms to keep them warm, somehow overbalanced and, legs and arms flailing, fell off the board and into the pool with an almighty splash. The trouble was, I was right next to Mrs le Bon, and when I surfaced, spluttering, it was to see that Mrs le Bon was nearly as wet as I was. Her slinky white dress was extra slinky – practically see-through, in fact, and her hair had lost all its bounce and fatness and was flat to the sides of her head.

She stood there for a moment in outraged and horrified silence; the only sound was her dripping on to the tiled floor. I stared back at her, trying to look sorrowful and penitent and at the same time keep up my doggy-paddle. It was difficult.

'Out!' she said when she could speak. 'All of you – out!'

We climbed out of the pool silently; I didn't dare look at anyone in case I started giggling in sheer horror.

'Sorry,' Annabel mumbled, unable to look us in the eye. 'You'd better go.'

We went into the cabins in silence and I beckoned to Fleur to come in with me.

'God!' I said in a horrified whisper. 'What d'you think of her, then?'

She shook her head, eyes wide. 'Wasn't it awful! Poor Annabel!' She looked at me sideways, 'Mind you, you making her mum a contestant for the Wet T-Shirt Competition can't have helped much.'

I stuffed my hand into my mouth to stop any giggles getting out. 'I couldn't help it!' I said, muffled. 'I just over-balanced!'

'Oh yeah?!' Fleur said.

'Poor Annabel, though . . .'

'Poor *rich* Annabel,' Fleur said thoughtfully.

Fleur's mum arrived to take her and a couple of others who lived in her direction, home, and the rest of us got dry as quickly as we could and walked to the bus stop together to catch the bus back.

Cerise sat next to me on the bus. She'd lost the pink glittering hearts – they were probably floating in the pool – but she was still wearing electric blue mascara, only now it had been transformed into electric blue streaks running down her face.

'Well!' she said, 'how about that, then?'

'How about it!' I echoed.

'Money isn't everything, is it?' she said in a wise voice scrubbing at her face with a tissue. 'Of course, Annabel's an only child, you see – just like me. It's so difficult for us.' She smiled at me sweetly. 'Mickey, I was wondering if you'd like me to come round and see you one evening?'

I looked at her, startled. 'What for?' I asked.

'Does it have to be *for* something?' she asked. 'I just thought it would be nice for some of us to see something of each other in the evenings. I could come to tea if you like.'

'Well, yes, I'spose so,' I said, wondering how I was going to stand a whole evening of Cerise.

'I'd like to meet your family,' she went on, 'as I said, I'm an only child, so Mummy's always saying how nice it would be for me to have a friend who's got brothers and sisters.'

'Oh, well, er ... come round when you want, then,' I said lamely.

'Can I really?' she said. 'I'll come when everyone's at home, shall I? When's that likely to be?'

'Friday, I suppose,' I said doubtfully. 'My brothers' friends sometimes come round then and they rehearse in the garage.'

'Right!' she beamed. 'I'll be there next Friday!'

'Great,' I said, not actually meaning great, meaning *Oh no.* What on earth would we talk about? Boys and hairdos and electric blue mascara, I supposed.

When I got home Mum wanted to know all about Annabel's house and the swimming pool and everything, and somehow I just couldn't bring myself to mention Mrs le Bon and the slight accident I'd caused, so I just told her about the conservatory and the changing-rooms and the tropical plants – all the bits she wanted to know.

'There!' she said with satisfaction when I'd finished. 'Didn't I tell you you'd meet all sorts of interesting new friends at that school? Just think how nice it'll be next summer to have a friend with a pool! Why, you can spend all the holidays there!'

'Mmm. Maybe,' I said evasively. 'Er ... mum – I've got a friend who wants to come round next Friday.'

'Of course!' she said. She beamed at me. 'I've

been dying for you to bring one of your new friends home. It's Annabel, is it? You want to repay her hospitality. Well, we won't be able to offer swimming pools or . . .'

'No, it's Cerise,' I said.

She frowned. 'Which one's that?'

Well, the . . . er . . . pink one,' I said.

'Oh, how nice,' mum said vaguely.

Chapter Five
OPERATION ALISON

Cerise was waiting for me in the playground the following Friday morning.

'Got everything?' I asked her as I got off the bus.

'Of course!' she said. She had pink plastic heart-shaped slides in her hair, but they didn't do anything to keep it from frizzing in a great big bush round her head. 'I've got my clothes to change into and my make-up bag and my best cassettes and . . .'

'I don't mean for tonight,' I said – I'd almost forgotten that she was supposed to be coming to tea – 'I mean for Operation Alison.'

'Oh – that!' she said, and we both looked round to make sure Alison wasn't anywhere near. She nodded. 'All in here!' she said, shaking her beauty box.

'Right!' I said. 'Let's get into class, then.'

Friday morning had been chosen as Getting Back at Alison morning. She'd been getting worse and worse; was always having nasty digs at people and pinching things whenever she found one of us on our own – it was getting so that a girl couldn't creep away and eat a sneaky bar of chocolate without Alison coming along and stealing it. So . . . we'd all worked out a plan and we put it into action in the classroom before Alison arrived. Alice was sent out to delay her on her way in.

Alison and Alice both arrived in class just a few seconds before Mrs Mackie did. She took the register, then asked us to get our rough books out of our desks because she had some notices to read out. We were all watching Alison, of course, and she lifted the lid of her desk, then shut it again very quickly, looking alarmed.

'I said rough books, please, Alison,' Mrs Mackie said, her eagle eye on Alison - she'd had her moved right to the front where she could see her. 'Get yours out, will you?'

Alison lifted her lid again, rummaged in the desk and then put the lid down.

'I can't find it,' she said, all red in the face and flabbergasted.

'Well, where is it, then?' Mrs Mackie asked, and, walking to stand beside Alison, she threw open her desk lid. Everyone craned to look although the whole class knew what was in there, of course: about sixty different things – packets of sweets, bars of chocolate, fizzy drinks, crisps, packets of biscuits, cartons of raisins, bags of peanuts – every single thing that Alison had taken from one of us during the weeks we'd been there had been duplicated and piled inside her desk. She had a whole miniature tuck shop in there.

'What on earth is all this?!' Mrs Mackie asked in astonishment. 'Where did all these things come from?'

Alison looked up at her, shocked and stunned. 'I don't know,' she said.

Mrs Mackie looked round the class. 'Has anyone else any idea?'

With our fingers crossed, we all shook our heads or murmured that we hadn't the faintest idea.

Mrs Mackie looked round the class slowly, then back at Alison. 'Hmm,' she said, 'I don't know what all this is about but I've rather been wondering about you, Alison. To my way of thinking you seem a bit too keen on using your er . . . rather dominant personality, shall we call it . . . to persuade other girls to let you have your own way. Are you sure you don't know how you came by these things?'

Alison shook her head dumbly.

'Then if they're not yours, perhaps you wouldn't mind distributing them round the class,' she said, and Alison, taking armfuls of sweets at a time, actually had to give them out to the rest of us while we all exchanged secret, gloating glances. It had worked like a dream. Maybe now she'd leave us alone.

In the playground at lunch time we all had another talk about the Revue – all except Alison. She kept a humpy distance from us and stayed talking to some second years by the sheds. I listened to all the others going on about what they were going to do and agonised again about what *I* could do for a turn. The night before I'd asked mum for ideas about things I was good at, and she'd said I was absolutely outstanding at treading on people's feet and making a mess of my room, how would they go down on stage? Jamie said I could do a fair turn at getting all the controls on the video wrong so that it never recorded what it was supposed to, and Paul said why didn't I appear as a girl who could break the entire contents of a model plane kit just by looking at it?

I gloomily told Fleur that I wasn't able to do anything, and she said why didn't I be a master of ceremonies?

'We need someone in charge! You could be backstage directing everyone else and telling them what order to go on and all that.'

'Wouldn't that be mistress of ceremonies?' Annabel asked.

'Well, whatever. I mean, we can't all be performers, can we?' Fleur said. 'Not all of us are good at things.'

'And someone's got to be in charge of the running order and make sure people turn up with the right clothes and everything,' Arina said.

'Mickey did think of having the Revue in the first place,' Jasbir added.

I beamed at everyone. 'If I'm master of ceremonies will I have to wear a spangled suit and a top hat?'

'I think that's a ringmaster,' Fleur giggled, and then she looked a bit miffed. 'Look, we've got Mickey fixed up, but what am I going to do?'

'Be assistant master of ceremonies?' Erica asked.

Fleur shook her head. 'I want something of my own. Maybe I could be the Amazing Fat Girl . . . roll up, roll up – come and marvel at how one girl can be so big . . .' A wide smile suddenly came over her face, 'No, I know!'

'What?' we all asked.

'We can't have a sponsored swim, so why don't I do a sponsored *slim*?!'

She looked round at us excitedly. 'Everyone's always going on about me being fat, but every time they say anything it makes me twice as determined to stay as I am. If I choose to do it for myself, though, for the charity shield . . .'

'Great!'I said. Although I'd got used to Fleur being fat, it would be much nicer to have her ordinary-sized, even just to stop toads like Alison having goes at her all the time.

It was all decided, then, and just about everyone – or everyone who wanted one – had jobs to do for the Revue. Arina and Jasbir weren't going to be allowed to do a dance, so they were going to paint the posters advertising the Revue and make the tickets. We were going to go all out for it, we decided; we'd show Mrs Mackie that it wasn't just her wonderful, marvellous last lot of first years who could win the Charity Shield.

Mum came to meet Cerise and me from school and I think she was a bit surprised at the sight of Cerise in white high-heeled boots with a pink satin bow stuck on the back of her head. Cerise had also – magically – grown a bust from somewhere. I thought it must have sprung up overnight, but Fleur said that she had to be wearing a padded bra, 'With two socks down it as well, by the look of her,' she'd added.

'Are you changing?' Cerise asked as soon as we got to my house, and I said I might put on jeans later, when I could be bothered. She wanted to go and get changed straight away, though, so we went up to my room and she put on a pink blouse with stand-up collar and a tight, stretchy mini-skirt with a very wide – *very very* wide – black elastic belt. As well as this she applied the four different sorts of smells and a load of pink eye shadow which made her look like an albino rabbit. When all this was done she wanted to go and be introduced to Jamie and Paul but, knowing full well what their reaction would be and being dead embarrassed at even walking downstairs with her, I pretended they had loads of school work and didn't like being interrupted. We stayed in my room instead and she did the cancan for me. Again.

When Mum called out that tea was ready we went down. I had to hand it to mum, even when she saw Cerise all done up she restrained herself and carried on as normal – as if she often had a Madonna look-alike to tea, but when Jamie and Paul appeared and saw her in all her glory they nearly fell over backwards.

'Hi, boys!' Cerise said, and she lowered her head and fluttered pink eyelashes at them.

Jamie and Paul muttered something awful and we all sat down to eat pizza. During the pizza, Cerise entertained us with stories about her clothes – where she bought them, what she liked to do on Saturdays (go shopping) and how very much she'd like to have brothers.

'Especially two like you,' she cooed, and Jamie and Paul practically disappeared into the carpet.

'Now, what are your birth signs?' she said when we were clearing away, and Jamie didn't know his and Paul didn't care. She found out what they were, though, and – what d'you know? – although Paul was Aries and Jamie was Aquarius they were both absolutely compatible with *her* sign. 'Isn't that uncanny?' she said, 'the four of us should really get along!' And I don't know how she worked *that* out because she hadn't even asked *my* birthday.

She had a weird view about brothers and sisters – she seemed to think that we spent time in each other's company. More than that – that we actually *talked* to each other. When everything was cleared away and Jamie and Paul were just about to disappear like they usually did, she announced that she'd brought a hip-hop cassette with her.

'Shall I put it on?' she asked, 'and then we can clear some of the furniture away and do some dancing.'

Of course, you couldn't see Jamie for dust. One minute he was standing there, the next I heard his bedroom door slam.

Paul wasn't quite so quick. 'I've . . . er . . . got work to do . . .' he said, edging towards the door.

Cerise boogied up to him, humming under her breath. 'Oh come on!' she said, 'just one little dance!'

'Honest!' he said, 'lotsawork . . . Monday . . . deadline . . . sorry.'

And then there was a faint blur as he ran for the door and we heard his bedroom door slam and the key turning in the lock.

'Oh!' Cerise pouted. 'I thought we'd all spend the evening together.'

'We do sometimes,' I said. And then I thought about it. 'Christmas, for instance.'

'Well, what time will the other boys be round?' she wanted to know, 'the rest of the group?'

'About eight,' I said. 'They won't let you in the garage, though. They won't let *anyone* in.'

She pouted again, then sighed heavily. 'I've got this little song and dance act, you see . . .'

'The cancan?' I asked fearfully. I'd seen it so many times I could do it in my sleep.

'No, not the cancan. Another one. And I was thinking that if they saw it they might like me to do a few numbers with them. When they get to be famous and go on stage, that is.'

I stared at her, wondering how one girl could be so mistaken. 'I don't think they'd like that . . .' I said tentatively. Talk about the understatement of the year.

'Oh, but I'm really good! Mummy says she's going to get me on a TV talent show with it! All the groups have girl singers now, you know. They're all the go.'

'I don't think . . .'

'I'll just show you how it goes, shall I? And then you can tell them about it.'

'Right,' I said faintly.

'I've got a little sequinned top – I'll go and put it on, shall I?'

'If you like,' I said. If she ever wanted to come home with me again I'd say my brothers had moved out . . .

Chapter Six
TROUBLED WATERS

The following Tuesday we were let out for Break after a particularly horrible maths lesson, so though it was cold out – we'd moved into our duffle coats -it was nice to get away from Mrs Taylor, who was dead strict.

We all moved off in a straggly group towards the library, which was in one of those buildings which are supposed to be temporary but aren't really. We always hung around the library. It was funny, every year from the Fifth downwards had special places to go in the playground and they more or less stuck to them. Did everyone move round a place each year, I wondered? When we were second years would we take over the place by the sheds? Only the Sixth didn't have to come out and freeze like the rest of us – they had their own lounging-about place in the Sixth form block with their own coffee machine and everything.

We were just talking about the Revue and sorting out when our first rehearsal would be when Jasbir appeared round the library building, looking excited.

'I've just been for a walk and guess what I've seen!'

'Something boring, I expect,' Arina said straight away. The two of them were awful, they never stopped ratting at each other.

'It wasn't boring, actually,' Jasbir said, turning her back on Arina. 'It was very extremely interesting.'

'What then?' Arina asked.

'Mrs Potter talking to a policeman!'

'What's so great about that?' someone asked.

'Just that he looked very cross. Furious!'

Philippa appeared out of nowhere. 'Is he still there? Where are they?'

'In the car park!' Jasbir said. 'You go and look.'

While Philippa had gone to have a spy we discussed what it might be, and wondered briefly if perhaps Mrs Potter was planning to run off with him. Philippa arrived back, breathless, and we formed a small crowd around her.

'I think he's come to arrest her!' she said dramatically. 'They're in the car park and he's pointing at something and she looks really upset.'

'Really!' I said, and we all chewed it over a bit and then Jasbir and I ran over to tell Su, who'd only just come out.

'Guess what?!' we said, 'Mrs Potter's being arrested!'

'Really?! Whatever for?' Su asked, her mouth going into a great big 'O'.

Jasbir and I looked at each other and shrugged. 'Don't know,' I said, 'something to do with a driving offence, we think.'

'Perhaps she hasn't paid a parking fine?' Su suggested.

We both shook our heads. 'It's more serious than that,' Jasbir said. 'You should see how angry he looks.'

'Absolutely raving,' I agreed.

'Did he have handcuffs?' Su asked breathlessly.

'Think so,' Jasbir said.

'Sure to have done,' I added.

The news spread like wildfire right round the library and, with a little help from Philippa, to the third years, the next group along the playground to us, who always stood near the gate – all the better to see any stray boys from the school next door. At the end of Break we went in, still talking about it, and one of the third years asked me if I'd been the actual person who'd seen 'Mrs Potter being taken away.'

'Not exactly,' I said, 'but one of my class did.

Almost taken away, anyway,' I amended, 'the policeman was just about to . . .'

'She knocked someone down on a zebra crossing, I heard,' the girl said excitedly. 'Disgusting, isn't it? She drove off without stopping.'

'Terrible!' I said.

On the way in I was stopped by a first year girl in Mrs Clark's, the other first-year class. 'Apparently Mrs Potter was seen being pulled into the back of a police van,' she whispered. 'She was kicking and screaming, they said.'

'Fancy!' I said. Someone else must have actually seen her go, then . . . I rushed over to tell Fleur.

We walked briskly through school to our next class, the news about Mrs Potter going down and along the corridors even faster than we were. When we got to the computer room – we were having Computer Logic – Miss Philby hadn't arrived, so we sat down and Philippa went out the front to tell us what else she'd found out about Mrs Potter. She'd been the last one to see her, of course, and she had all the latest information.

'Apparently she's been arrested and is going straight to Scotland Yard!' she said, and when we all oohed and ahhed, added, 'Well, after knocking down three children I'm not surprised! Apparently they've been hunting for her for weeks. They've investigated every red car in England.'

'But her car's blue!' Su said.

'Well . . . whatever,' Phillippa shrugged. 'I can't remember the details.'

'Who knew all these extra bits, then?' I asked.

But Philippa didn't seem to know. 'News just sort-of came in,' she said vaguely. 'Every time I spoke to someone they knew a bit more.'

'I heard she'd been put in a straitjacket!' Arina said. 'Apparently the police have to do that in the case of dangerous criminals.'

I tried hard to think of Mrs Potter – our small, chubby, music teacher, as a dangerous criminal. It was difficult.

'A third year told me that she'd heard that Mrs Potter had knocked down ten children in a nursery school class on a zebra . . .' Annabel began excitedly, but she had to stop because Miss Harmer, the head, swept majestically into the room.

Philippa slipped to her place and we stopped jabbering and got to our feet immediately, as had been rammed into us by Mrs Mackie.

'Miss Philby is ill,' she explained, while we all tried to look instantly clean, tidy and good, 'so you won't be having Computer Logic. You won't be bored, though, because we happen to have an interesting visitor in school.'

And then before we could draw breath Mrs Potter came in – followed by a policeman. *The* policeman.

'PC Compton is a family friend of Mrs Potter's,' Miss Harmer said, her eyes ranging up and down the class for earrings, traces of make-up and jumpers which weren't as red as they should be, 'and he's very kindly offered to come in to talk to you.'

No one moved or even breathed. Mrs Potter moved front stage and beamed at us. 'I'd like to introduce PC Compton,' she said. 'He's going to give a very interesting talk entitled "The Schoolgirl and the Environment" which I know you'll find absolutely fascinating.'

Fleur scribbled something on her rough book and slid it over to me: *Not half as fascinating as having you clapped in irons and carted off to prison . . .*

It wasn't fascinating, of course, in fact we were rather subdued when we went out to lunch. And we avoided being in a group in case any of the other years tried to get hold of us and question us about what had actually and truthfully been seen.

After lunch we had history in our own classroom with Mrs Mackie. After she'd called our names she asked Alice to take the register back to Mrs Green's office and then told us to get out our text-books. She rummaged around in her desk for a bit and then she muttered something about having forgotten to get some papers about that day's lesson.

'Mr Waters was looking at them for me and

I meant to get them back from him at lunch time,' she said.

I sprang into action. 'Shall I go and get them for you?' I asked. Well, now that I was MC for the Revue I'd decided to try and change my image; I wanted Mrs Mackie and the rest of the teachers to take me more seriously. I didn't want to be class boffin, like Alice, but neither did I want to be known as the girl who dropped things, trod on everyone's feet and generally got things wrong.

'I don't know,' Mrs Mackie said doubtfully. 'Do you know where Mr Waters' office is?'

'Of course,' I said.

'It's rather difficult to find and the papers are very important . . .' Her eyes scanned the class, 'Perhaps I'd better ask someone else.'

I stood up. 'Mrs Mackie,' I said in a very dignified way, 'I will find Mr Waters' office and get the papers back to you straight away. I'll be back before you've even noticed I've gone.'

'Well,' Mrs Mackie said slowly and reluctantly, 'I suppose it'll be all right.'

Smiling broadly, I made for the door.

'Mr Waters is a little old-fashioned, so don't go in if he's got someone with him, will you? Knock first and wait until he tells you to come in.'

'Of course,' I said.

'Now, you know where Mr Waters' office is, do you? Turn right at the school entrance, past the gym and the art room, turn left at the third corridor and carry on . . .'

'I know exactly,' I said, hardly listening. Of course I knew where to go – I'd been at Park Wood for weeks . . . everyone knew their way around the school by now.

I zipped past the gym and along the corridor, humming to myself and thinking about the running order for the Revue. Although we were all sick to death of Cerise and her cancan, it did look like being a rip-roaring number to finish with. Or should we start on a rip-roarer to get everyone sitting up in their seats? I couldn't decide – but then a person of power always does have difficult decisions to make. It was probably just the same for all those famous producers in Hollywood . . .

I reached Mr Waters' office: a small door right at the end of a corridor, and knocked.

I waited patiently but there was no reply, so I pressed my ear to the door and knocked again. I thought I could faintly hear the drone of voices, so he must be interviewing. I wasn't sure what he did – some sort of school financial business or something – all I knew was that he was very old and very grumpy.

I strode up and down outside for a while, then I knocked again. Still no reply. I mentally started listing Revue turns in my head: cancan, violin, comedy sketch, magician, imitations, another comedy bit. . . Paula and Sammy were doing a Victoria Wood sketch which no one had seen because they couldn't rehearse it without having hysterics at the first line.

I knocked again. Mrs Mackie would think I'd got lost. That or I'd dropped all the papers en route and they'd blown away. What was the stupid man doing all this time? Why couldn't he stop it and ask me to come in?

I stuck my ear to the door again but I couldn't hear anything. Maybe he'd bored his visitor to death and then gone to sleep. I looked at my watch: it was nearly ten minutes into the lesson – Mrs Mackie would be going loony. Should I put my head round the door? She'd specifically said not to go in unless he asked me, though. Suppose he wasn't there? Should I go back and ask her if I should go in? No, she'd just sigh loudly, say she might have known I couldn't get it right, and send Alice along instead.

I knocked very loudly indeed – so loudly that I almost frightened myself. Still nothing – and no voices, either. Suppose he hadn't bored his visitor to death, suppose he was dead himself? Suppose I went in there and he was slumped on the desk, dead as a doormat? In that case, should I go back and tell Mrs Mackie or would I have to go straight to Miss Harmer? If I decided on Miss Harmer would she notice that I'd tried to take in my skirt a bit and it had gone all wavy?

I tapped again. 'Mr Waters!' I called. I rattled the door handle a bit. Should I just peep round the door and take a tiny glimpse? If he was slumped on the desk I'd shut the door immediately; I didn't want to discover any bodies . . .

'Mr Waters, are you all right?' I said in a breathless whisper. I pushed open the door a fraction with a hand that was shaking. It was very dark; just how long had the body been there? Why hadn't the cleaners found him?

'Mr Waters!' I opened the door a little further. 'I've come from Mrs Mackie. She asked me to get . . .'

It was absolutely black in there and my heart was in my mouth as I groped for the light. I didn't think I was going to be very brave if I saw a dead body . . .

As the light went on two things happened: (a) I realised I'd been waiting outside the stationery cupboard and (b) I heard footsteps coming along the corridor.

'Whatever are you doing in here?' Mrs Mackie asked in astonishment. 'Mr Waters' office is at the bottom of the last corridor on the left!'

I stood in the middle of thousands of manila envelopes and school prospectuses, feeling stupid. 'I . . . er . . . thought I'd just check things were all right in here . . .'

'I've been looking everywhere for you.' She clicked off the light. 'Come along, I've seen Mr Waters and got the papers. With a bit of luck I might just have a few minutes of history left.'

Mrs Mackie walked briskly back along the corridor and I scuttled to try and keep up. All the time she was tutting gently to herself and shaking her head. 'Mr Waters' office!' she announced as we passed it. 'You know it's his because, surprisingly enough, it's the one that has his name on.'

'So it has,' I said, and smiled a sickly sort of smile.

Chapter Seven
CRIMEWATCH?

'Have I lost weight, d'you think?' Fleur asked. She pulled at the waistband of her school skirt and, by holding her tummy in as far as she could, managed to pull out the skirt and leave the tiniest little gap.

'Well . . .' I said doubtfully.

'I have! I'm sure I have. I've got loads of sponsors: all my aunties and my mum and dad's friends and my friends at home. I'm charging them a penny for each pound I lose.' She sat back on the bench and looked down at her lunch: a lettuce leaf, a piece of cheese and a squashy-looking tomato. 'The little scraps that I'm eating . . . I must be losing something.'

'Oh, you are,' I said, pretending to be convinced. 'Now I look at you closely, I can see the weight's positively falling off.'

'Really?' she asked, pleased.

'Definitely.'

'Enough to stop Alison shouting "Fatty Fleur" after me all the time?'

'Of course,' I said. I stood up. 'If you've finished pushing that lettuce leaf round your plate, we're supposed to be having a rehearsal,' I said. 'Coming to watch?'

'If it means not having to go out in the cold – yes,' she said.

We went into the music room, which Mrs Mackie had arranged for us to use a couple of lunchtimes a week. When the Revue actually happened, of course, we'd be in the school theatre – but that was the dining hall at lunch time so we couldn't rehearse in it.

I was beginning to regret being MC. I'd wanted to do something for the Revue – yes – but I think it might have been easier to juggle sixteen teachers in the air or abseil up the side of the school building. At rehearsals I was supposed to sort everyone out, you see, but no one *wanted* to be sorted. All they ever wanted to do was to show off their own particular turn and have everyone else look at them, so all a rehearsal was, was sixteen girls all doing their own things all at the same time as loudly as they could.

It was only when it came to trying to sort out who was going to go on stage for the actual performance that they all got shy: everyone had refused point blank to go first – even Cerise.

When Fleur and I arrived in the music room it was like a bear garden. Donna was doing conjuring tricks at the same time as keeping up a loud commentary on how extremely magical she was; Su, magician's assistant, was sitting on the floor shrieking with laughter and trying to squirm herself into a leotard with sequins sewn on it (she wasn't exactly thin, either – she'd told us that if people didn't turn up for their takeaways, she ate them), Sammy and Paula were rolling round in hysterics over their Victoria Wood act, Annabel and Philippa were tap-dancing (Philippa was shouting 'Look, look at me, everyone!') and Cerise was stuffed into yards and yards of pink frills and – well, I don't have to say what she was doing. The only one who was seriously rehearsing was Alice, sitting quietly in the corner looking at her music and playing her violin. No one could hear her, though.

Well, there was nothing I, as master of ceremonies and officially in charge, could do, so I picked up Donna's toy rabbit-out-of-a-hat and Fleur and I started throwing it backwards and forwards to each other.

In the middle of all this Mrs Mackie appeared, striding in and clapping her hands. As the rabbit whistled past her left ear, everyone stopped what they were doing apart from Alice, who played on quietly and unknowingly as a sort of background accompaniment to Mrs Mackie's complaints.

'We can hear you from the staff room!' she said. 'The other teachers asked if it could possibly be my first years who are making all this row, and I was quite indignant. As I came closer, though, I was horrified to find out that it *is* you.'

We all stood about scuffling our feet. 'Now, who's in charge?' Mrs Mackie asked briskly.

No one moved, but they all looked in my direction.

'Not *you*, Michelle?' Mrs Mackie asked, clearly shocked. 'No wonder the place is in uproar.'

'We . . . er . . . haven't got things quite sorted out yet,' I said.

'I can see that and it doesn't look as if you *are* going to get things sorted. What you need is a teacher in here with you.'

Everyone's faces fell.

'No, honestly!' I said quickly. 'We'll be perfectly all right. We . . . er . . . wouldn't want to take a member of staff from their lunch break.' I assumed a kind and thoughtful face,'Not when they get so little free time.' I appealed to everyone else, 'We wouldn't want to mess up a teacher's lunch, would we?'

'Certainly not,' several voices said.

'That's all very well,' Mrs Mackie said, 'but as your class teacher I really feel that . . .'

Suddenly, over the wails of Alice's violin, came the clear voice of Miss Harmer outside.

'I'm looking for Mrs Mackie. Most annoying . . . can't find her anywhere.'

Mrs Mackie frowned – it was a well known fact that she and Miss Harmer hated each other. 'I've got to go,' she said, 'but understand – if this terrible row happens at lunch time ever again you'll have to be supervised.'

'*Where has she got to*?' came from outside. *'This is really most inconvenient . . .'*

Mrs Mackie set her lips in a straight line and went out, and we all looked at each other and sighed with relief.

'Saved by Miss Harmer!' Annabel said.

'Saved by *Erica*!' Erica corrected, coming in at the door where Mrs Mackie had gone out.

'What d'you mean?' I asked.

She grinned. 'Pretty good imitation of Miss Harmer, don't you think? It got rid of Mrs Mackie for you, anyway . . .'

Last period that day was games. Games weren't all that popular – not with Fleur and me, anyway – but having them last period was really bad because it meant we had to shower and struggle, half dry, back into our clothes before the buses arrived to take us home.

The school field was being used by some hockey-playing fifth years so we were set a circuit to run: round the school, in and out of the portables, past the sheds and finishing up in the playground where Miss Hermitage had set up some jolly obstacles for us to jump over.

After a couple of circuits, somehow I went slightly wrong and ended up at the back of the school car park. I wasn't worried; I decided I'd let the others run round the school a few more times and then I'd casually run up and join them, all nice and fresh.

I dawdled by the wall, amusing myself by looking at the cars and trying to guess which teacher had what. I'd just put Mrs Mackie down for something sturdy, plain and reliable in grey when I saw a strange figure lurking near a newish, sporty car parked under the trees. Now, one thing that boring talk on 'The Schoolgirl and the Environment' had taught us was that we all had to become more aware of our surroundings and especially of what was going on right under our eyes. We had to really look at things, notice details, *observe* – that way we could help prevent crime and save the world. Or so the policeman had said.

So, I stood there, keenly observing, while the man, a villainous character if ever I saw one, walked all round the car and looked it up and down, then glanced all round him in a suspicious manner and tried the handle. It was locked, but that didn't deter him – he walked to the other side and tried the passenger door handle, then he tried the boot and *then* started looking underneath. All the time he was doing this he was casting quick, nervous glances towards the school buildings and sort-of sinking down as far as he could into his turned-up coat collar.

I happened to know the car belonged to Miss Lemming, our art teacher, because I'd seen her driving in one morning in a red dress which matched it, and thought how trendy she looked. The art room wasn't far away; just about near enough to slip over and warn her that a seedy-looking individual was about to break into her car and make off with it . . .

Keeping close to the ground and using the other cars for cover, I slunk off towards the school, going past the sheds so I wouldn't have to touch the playground and be seen by Miss Hermitage. Just as I disappeared, shadow-like, into the building, the thief was trying the car boot again.

Miss Lemming, luckily, had a free period and was in the art room stacking easels.

'Thank goodness!' I said. 'You've got to come quickly. There's someone in the car park trying to steal your car!'

'What?!' she said.

'A man. Real criminal sort of face like you see on the photofits,' I said breathlessly. 'Shall we ring the police or just get out there?'

She looked flustered. 'Oh dear! We'll go out there, I think,' she said. 'Just the fact of someone appearing might be enough to scare him off – and the police could be ages getting here.'

'He may be armed . . .' I murmured.

'What?!'

'Well, you never know,' I said. 'In this talk on "The Schoolgirl and the Environment" we were told never to tackle anyone . . .'

'I'm not going to tackle him,' she said, 'I'm just going to run out there and try and frighten him. Quickly!'

We rushed down the corridor then outside and across the playground. In the excitement I'd forgotten all about Miss Hermitage until I crossed right in front of her obstacles.

She shouted at me in surprise and then called, 'Michelle Young! Where have you been? Come here immediately!'

I took no notice, just ran on bravely. It would be all right once she knew what I'd been doing; the whole school would have reason to be grateful to me.

'Take care!' I urged Miss Lemming as we ran. 'He looked a real villain.'

'Don't worry,' she said. 'Those types are often cowards when it comes to head-on confrontations.'

'Not him!' I said darkly. 'He looked as if he'd stab you soon as look at you . . .'

We turned the corner and reached the car park. 'Okay!' she shouted. 'Let's be having him!'

The man was still there looking deeply criminal and suspicious, and was actually *leaning* on Miss Lemming's car.

'There!' I yelled, as Miss Lemming stopped in her tracks.

'Miss Lemming, there he is!' I shouted.

She started running again – right up to him and flung her arms round him. 'Darling!' she said to the suspicious criminal. 'I didn't know you'd be back today!'

'I thought you said you'd leave the car open,' the suspicious criminal said, clearly niggled. 'That or hide the key somewhere.'

'I forgot! I wouldn't be out here now except that one of my girls came and told me that . . .' She turned to me. 'Mickey! I just don't understand, I really don't. How could you think that my fiancé was a . . .'

'Oh I didn't mean *this* gentleman!' I said. 'Not at all . . . of course not. Good afternoon, Mr . . . er . . .'

He just looked at me coldly so I pointed into the distance, squinting my eyes.

'*There* he goes!' I said. 'Look, he's getting away!' Miss Lemming and the suspicious criminal looked, but of course they didn't see anything.

'Just missed him! What a shame!' I said. 'He ran round the corner and got away. Oh dear . . .'

And moving swiftly away, not having saved the school, I went to face Miss Hermitage.

Chapter Eight
THE FACTS OF LIFE

'How are Jamie and Paul?' Cerise asked one morning as we went into class. She hesitated by my locker, 'I was thinking of having a little party on my birthday . . . I wondered if you'd like to come and bring them with you.'

I smiled in what I hoped was a kind way – mostly at the thought of *me* bringing *them* anywhere. 'Quite honestly, Cerise, I don't think they'd be interested,' I said. 'They've got their own friends, you see. They wouldn't come to any parties given by my friends.'

'Not even me? I mean, I'm practically in the pop music world like they are.'

'Not even you,' I said. *Especially* not you, I meant. Jamie and Paul hadn't recovered yet, and didn't want to meet any of my friends now. I'd had Fleur over for the evening a couple of weeks ago and though I'd told them both that Fleur wasn't the slightest bit interested in them, they'd refused to come in. They'd gone for a pizza and then hidden at a mate's house until the coast was clear.

Cerise pouted. 'Boys can be cruel, can't they?' she said sadly, moving off in a slow and heartbroken way.

After Register we had PSD, which we all liked. PSD stood for Personal and Social Development and though Mrs Mullins, who took us, wasn't all that young, she was quite trendy and a bit of a laugh. Another thing we liked about her lesson was that she didn't take it sitting out the front at her table, but came and sat on our desks and chatted to us as if it was break and we were all having a friendly chat.

We talked about all sorts of things: hygiene and periods and how not to have smelly feet and how often you should wash your hair, all that sort of thing, as well as how to answer the phone and how to introduce people say, if you're out with your mum and a teacher comes up. Cerise kept wanting to talk about going out on dates with boys but Mrs Mullins would say breezily, 'Lots of time later on for all that business, Cerise!' and Cerise would then ask what sort of false eyelashes Mrs Mullins recommended or something equally daft.

Actually, Cerise only came to the first few

PSD lessons because after that she – and Alison – had to go for extra tuition in Maths and English at those times. No one was surprised at Cerise going but we were surprised – and pleased – that Alison had to go as well. We liked getting rid of *her*.

This particular afternoon PSD was all about getting on with our families and being prepared to help out in the house where necessary. Also, as Donna's mum had just had a baby, a bit about pregnancy and new babies. We all tried to be frightfully grown up here and not giggle when she started talking about below the waist bits.

We couldn't get much out of Mrs Mullins in the way of interesting facts of life, though, and afterwards Philippa let us know that she found it all terribly childish.

'Honestly, Mrs Mullins treats us as if we were eight!' she said. 'Every time I asked her a question about reproduction she just said we'd be doing it in biology. I can't see why she can't *say*.'

None of us said anything so she added, 'Anyway, I know it all. I know everything.'

This was nothing new – Philippa always thought she knew everything.

'I've known all about it for years,' she went on loftily.

'How come there's things you wanted to ask, then?' Fleur said.

Philippa sniffed and didn't reply. 'I bet I

know more than all of you about things like that,' she said. 'I know all sorts of things about babies and sex and everything.'

Everyone started to move off towards our next lesson, not really taking much interest.

'And I know a real big secret, as well!' Philippa said loudly. 'I bet no one else in this class knows it. No one in this school!'

'What then?' I asked, falling for it. A few of the others looked round, just in case it was anything worth hearing.

'Someone . . . someone in the third year . . . is . . . guess what?'

'Someone is guess what?' Erica said, 'how interesting.'

'Someone's having a baby!' said Philippa triumphantly.

Those who had turned away turned swiftly back, those who had wandered off stopped in their tracks.

'See!' she said. 'I told you you'd be amazed!'

'I don't believe you,' I said.

'You didn't believe me about what was in the poison cupboard!'

We all stared at her. Could she be right?

'She'd be taken away . . . she'd be in a special home or something,' Alice said. 'They wouldn't just let her stay here.'

'They would because no one else knows about it yet.'

'How do you know, then?' Erica asked.

'One break last week I heard her telling her friend,' Philippa said. She looked round at our disbelieving faces, 'I *did* hear her! Anyway, you can see just from looking at her.'

'We'll go and have a look at lunchtime!' Fleur said.

So at lunchtime we went in the dining hall first, and then a group of us gathered outside by the library.

'We'll just go and see what we think,' Erica said. 'Where can we find her? What's she look like?'

'She's small – or she *was* small,' Philippa said meaningfully. 'She's got blonde hair shaved right up the back – the way Mrs Mackie says we're not allowed to have it – and a funny face with a turned up nose.'

'I know her!' I said. 'She's sometimes on my bus.'

I led them off and we all went and huddled behind one of the bike sheds near the school gates and peered round it at the group of third years lounging against the wall.

'There she is!' said Philippa, pointing at the blonde girl, and we all stared very hard at her tummy. It was difficult because she was wearing a duffle coat and, though it was open, it kept flapping around.

'I don't think she looks fat,' Erica said after a moment. 'She looks quite normal to me. Skinny, if anything.'

'Rubbish!' Philippa said. 'You can see from the way she's standing . . . and she's got her hands in front of her tummy. My cousin used to stand just like that when she was pregnant.'

'If everyone who put their hands in front of their tummy was pregnant,' Su said, 'then my dad would be.'

Everyone laughed and the third years looked round at us.

'Who do you lot of kids think you're looking at?' one of them asked. 'Shouldn't you be going for your afternoon naps?'

'Run along, babies!' another one said.

'*Babies*!' we all repeated, and smiled at each other meaningfully.

We hung about the gate pretending to play feet off ground, all the time staring over at the blonde girl.

'Who do they think they're looking at?' she said indignantly after a while. 'Have I grown an extra nose or something?'

'I expect one of them's got a crush on you,' her friend said. 'You know how daft the first years are.'

We gathered into a little knot. 'What d'you think?' Jasbir asked excitedly. 'She might be . . .'

'Of course she is,' Philippa said. 'She's definitely got that sort of look about her.'

'If she is we ought to tell Mrs Mackie,' Alice said as we went in for the afternoon register.

She'd come along with us to look without really knowing what she was going for. 'She'd want to know something as important as that. It's our duty to tell.'

'We can't tell anyone,' I said. 'Not unless we definitely know it's true. Imagine the fuss there'd be if it wasn't.'

'It *is* true,' Philippa insisted, 'but no one can tell anyone because I'd get into trouble. It would be bound to come out that it was me who'd told you all.'

'Well, I really think we ought to tell someone,' Alice said in a worried voice. 'I'm sure my sister would tell.'

'Someone will have to go and have a good, long look before we do anything,' Fleur said. 'One of us will have to go right up to her . . .'

'I'll go!' I offered, and before I could think of a good reason for going, someone gave me a push and I was on my way over. 'And don't all stare!' I hissed over my shoulder.

'What do you want?' the blonde girl asked in an unfriendly way. 'Why have you all been watching us?'

My mouth opened and closed a few times as I thought of and then discarded possible reasons. I smiled brightly. 'It's just that your duffle coat is . . . is so nice. It looks so much better than all the other ones. I wanted to get a new one, you see, so I was looking at it wondering where you got it.'

'You were *all* looking,' she said.

'Well, that's because we were all . . . er . . . wondering.'

'Don't be so ridiculous! This is just a normal coat.'

'I suppose you'd think it was an awful cheek if I asked to try it on,' I said humbly. 'If it's not too much trouble, that is. I'd really like to see what it looked like on me.'

'You're loony!' the blonde girl said. 'If you think . . .'

'Oh, for goodness sake let her!' her friend said. 'We might get rid of them then. How can we talk properly with that lot hanging about and spying on us?'

The blonde girl tutted and rolled her eyes and grudgingly took the duffle coat off. She handed it to me and, my eyes fixed on her tummy, I put it on, looked down at myself and made admiring noises, then handed it back.

'Thanks,' I said. 'I'm definitely having one the same!'

'She must be barmy . . .' I heard her say as I scuttled back.

'She didn't look very fat to me,' I said when I reached my friends. 'Did you all get a good look?'

'She was facing in the wrong direction,' Arina said.

'You told us not to look!' Fleur added.

So we were none the wiser and I'd got a reputation amongst the third years for being an escaped loony. It didn't seem worth it, really.

Three days later – three days of Philippa telling us everything she knew about schoolgirl mothers – we had another PSD lesson.

'Mrs Mullins is Welfare as well as being a teacher,' Fleur said before the lesson, 'so if anyone knows about this girl, *she* will. I'm going to drop a broad hint about girls having babies when they're too young, and see if she picks it up.'

'Well, don't say I said anything!' Philippa said, all panicky. 'I don't want to be connected with it. I could get into serious trouble.'

'You should have the courage of your convictions,' said Alice loftily. 'If it's really true you should be prepared to stand up and say so.'

Getting the conversation round to having babies was easy enough, and then Fleur said casually that she'd heard that schoolgirl mothers were on the increase – did Mrs Mullins realise that?

'I'm sure they *are* on the increase,' Mrs Mullins said, 'but luckily, not in this school!'

'Only we heard this rumour, see . . . about a girl in the third year who might be . . . you know . . .' Fleur said, while we all nudged each other.

'Well, if it was anyone in the third year I'm sure I'd have heard by now,' Mrs Mullins said, 'because my daughter's a third year girl and she tells me all the gossip – everything going!'

We all must have looked stunned at this because she went on, 'Didn't you know? Mind you, she doesn't look anything like me – luckily for her! She's got blonde hair in one of those dreadful shaved-up-the-back haircuts – I think Miss Harmer only lets her get away with it because I teach here.'

There was a stunned silence, during which we all nudged each other again and looked over at Philippa, then Erica started laughing so much that she had to go out.

'Well, that's disposed of teenage mothers,' Mrs Mullins said pleasantly. 'And now I think we'll have a little chat about personal grooming and whether it's really necessary to shave our legs.'

Outside, waiting for the buses to go home, everyone gathered round Philippa.

'You made the whole thing up!' Fleur said. 'You just made it up to get attention!'

'I did not!' Philippa said hotly. 'I . . . I must have got it wrong, that's all. I misheard what she said.'

'How can you mishear someone saying they were expecting a baby?' Erica wanted to know.

'Well . . . er . . . I thought she said she was having a baby, but she must have said she was having . . . something else.'

'What? A cake for tea? A new pair of socks? Oh yes, that's almost the same!' Arina said.

'I won't believe another thing you say!' Erica said. 'Even if you tell me what day it is I'm going to check up!'

'Anyone can make a mistake,' Philippa muttered.

Chapter Nine
SWEET HOME ECONOMICS!

'Well, you've made a lovely job of these posters for your Revue,' Miss Lemming said, beaming at us – or beaming at the others, I should say; I hadn't got too many beams from her since the car park incident. 'These are exactly what you need to catch everyone's attention. They're very colourful, they give all the correct information and they tell people where to buy their tickets. I know the twins designed them but the rest of you had a lot to do with painting them, so well done all of you!'

'Arina only did a *little* bit of the design,' Jasbir said. 'Mostly it was my idea.'

'A little bit!' Arina exploded. 'I did nearly all of it! It was me who said to put that sparkly stuff at the top, and me who said to put a picture of the charity shield on it, and me who . . .'

'Well done *both* of you,' Miss Lemming said firmly. ' Now, who's going to put them up round the school? Not you, Michelle,' she added before I'd even put my hand up.

The posters were really good.

PARK WOOD FIRST YEARS PRESENT:
A GRAND REVUE IN AID OF
THE CHARITY SHIELD

was at the top, and then followed the names of everyone who was appearing and what they were doing, then came all the backstage people, and right at the bottom: *Mistress of Ceremonies: Michelle Young*.

'We'll have to have you designing and making the skiing trip posters,' Miss Lemming said. 'Miss Harmer will want those up at the beginning of next term.'

'I can ski already!' Cerise announced. 'I've been twice. I've got this all-in-one pink outfit with matching earmuffs. Mummy says I look just like a dear little bunny in it.'

We all laughed and then Fleur asked about skiing. 'Which years are allowed to go?' she wanted to know.

'Anyone who wants to in Lower School – first, second or third years.' Miss Lemming said. 'The older girls have a school trip to Sicily in the summer instead.'

'Where do we stay?' someone asked.

'In a huge hostel,' Miss Lemming said. 'There's usually about sixty girls and six or seven teachers.'

'Miss Harmer?' Cerise asked fearfully.

'Miss Harmer never goes,' Miss Lemming said with a smile. 'Lots of the others do, though. I always go and so does Mrs Mackie.'

'Does she actually go *skiing*?' I asked, trying to imagine Mrs Mackie, whom so far I'd only seen in frumpy beige crimplene outfits, in a fluorescent all-in-one go-faster ski suit.

'Of course. We're all pretty good at it, too.' She looked at our faces and laughed. 'We'll surprise you. We're all great fun when we're away from school!'

'Really?' I said, now trying to imagine Mrs Mackie whizzing down a ski run *and* Mrs Mackie being great fun – and failing both times. The ski trip sounded all right, though.

As well as the posters for the Revue we'd got together to make matching tickets, as well: complimentary ones for the school governors (Mrs Mackie said we had to) and Miss Harmer, but a pound for adults, 50p for children. As there were only a couple of weeks to go before the end of term we'd been allowed to sell the tickets in the dining-hall once a week. Not many of the girls in the other years bought them as they all had their own charity shield projects and weren't keen on giving money to *ours* but we sold plenty to teachers and the dinner ladies.

It was Fleur's and my turn to sell tickets and, knowing that Annabel hadn't bought any, I called her over and asked how many she wanted.

'You'll have to be quick!' Fleur said, rattling our cardboard box full of money at her. 'We might sell them all.'

'Yes, you never know – two hundred people might suddenly rush in here and clear us out!' I added.

Annabel shook her head. 'I don't want any,' she said. 'Well, not unless I have to have a ticket myself.'

'None?' I asked. 'Aren't your mum and dad coming?'

'I doubt it – they'll probably be away somewhere. And the housekeeper we've got now is new – she hardly knows me.'

'Well . . . d'you want one put by, just in case one of your parents is around?' I asked awkwardly, knowing how I'd hate it if no one turned up to see *me*.

She shook her head. 'Even if they were around they wouldn't come to a school event. It's not really my mum's sort of thing. "Darling, it's not really *us*," my mum will say.' She shrugged, 'I'm not even going to bother asking them.'

'But you're absolutely brilliant at tap dancing!' gushed Philippa by her side as usual. 'It's such a shame no one will be there to see you.'

'That's okay!' Annabel said. 'I'm used to it.' She laughed but it was a funny laugh. 'I expect they only sent me to tap-dancing classes in the first place to get rid of me.'

Philippa looked up at her hopefully. 'Why don't you come and stay with me on Revue night?' she asked. 'You won't want to go home all on your own, will you? My mum and dad wouldn't mind and it would be lovely to have you.'

'Could do,' Annabel said, looking quite pleased.

'Of course, my house isn't like yours,' Philippa went on in her creepy-crawly voice. 'I hope you wouldn't expect too much. I mean, yours is all huge and beautifully furnished and everything but I haven't even got a television in my room. And, well . . . I haven't even got my own bathroom either . . . I hope you won't mind.'

'Oh how dreadful . . . I can't bear it! No bathroom of your very own!' Fleur said.

Philippa turned to her indignantly. 'I'm just warning Annabel how *ordinary* people live,' she said.

'That's okay,' Annabel said with a grin, 'I don't mind slumming it occasionally.'

'No, of course you don't,' Philippa said humbly, not even realising that Annabel had been joking.

After lunch we had Home Economics, which was not one of my best subjects – but then, to be honest, I was still waiting to find a subject that I *was* best at. We'd done quite a lot of text book stuff in HE but this week was a practical; we were to make dainty titbits for the governors' and teachers' meeting that evening.

I was going to really try hard, I decided, to make something good. Or at least edible. I hadn't had much luck so far: the sponge cake I'd made a couple of weeks ago had turned out, as my darling brother Jamie had pointed out when he'd seen it, to look more like a washing up sponge than a Victoria sponge.

Mum had risen to defend me and said that just because I was a girl it didn't follow that I had to be good at domestic things; my skills might lie in other directions and what made him think he could make anything better? Of course, half an hour later, he came out of the kitchen with this very tall and very superior super-sponge that practically flew in on its own, it was so light.

Miss Attlee, HE teacher, sorted us into groups: savoury nibbles and sweet nibbles, pastry-based things and things-on-sticks. Fleur, Cerise and I were in one of the sweet nibble sections.

As we made our way over to our delegated corner of the kitchens, Cerise was looking very disgruntled. 'I don't want to do these stupid *petit fourses*,' Cerise said, looking at our ingredients and frowning. 'Alice's group have got all the luxurious stuff – the smoked salmon and everything. It's not fair!'

'I think it's down to who Miss Attlee trusts not to make a mess of the luxury items,' Fleur said. 'She just doesn't want those big fat prawns to end up on the floor.'

'We've got cherries, Cerise,' I said consolingly. 'Look, bright pink glacé cherries!'

'So we have,' she said, and cheered up.

'Now, we're only making very simple things so I think you're all sensible enough to get on on your own,' Miss Attlee said. 'I want to prepare the fruit punch for tonight so I'll be over by the sinks here chopping up apples and oranges. You've all got very clear and explicit directions on your wipe-clean recipe boards, so see if you can get on with them quietly.'

Our wipe-clean recipes weren't very exciting. Our group had to make little tiny biscuits – some with cherries on, some dipped in melted chocolate and nuts and some with a sort of blob of fondant stuck on top. I wanted to do the chocolate ones and, as Cerise had to have the cherry ones, Fleur was left with the fondant blobbies.

It seemed easy enough. We carefully mixed up the biscuit mixture, rolled it up in little balls and squashed it out a bit, then put the biscuits on trays ready to cook. There wasn't any room in the ovens, though, as they were full up with everyone else's vol-au-vents and sausages. We left our biscuits on the side while we licked round the bowls.

Fleur said she'd start making up her fondant while we were waiting, so Cerise started cutting up her cherries and I started melting my chocolate. I did it very slowly and carefully, putting it in a bowl over hot water just as the instructions said, but the thing was, I had a couple of little licks while it was melting, and then wiped my fingers round the edges where it had gone all up the bowl just to neaten it a bit, then sort-of dipped in further and further until, before I knew where I was, all the chocolate had gone. Just disappeared into thin air.

'D'you think Miss Attlee will notice if my biscuits have only got nuts on?' I asked Fleur, looking in the nut bag and taking a sample.

'D'you think she'll notice if my fondant blobs don't have any blobs?' she said, taking a few of my nuts.

'Where've they gone then?'

'The same place as your chocolate.'

We both suddenly looked over at Cerise: her mouth was all pink and sticky and she had a big smile on her face.

'Oh no!' Fleur said. 'All we're going to be making is small plain biscuits with no fancy bits!'

I looked up in alarm; Miss Attlee was coming over.

'Quick!' I said, 'pretend to be doing something. Roll out the biscuit mixture again.'

We grabbed the biscuit shapes from the tin trays and rolled it all together again just as Miss Attlee passed by on her way to the serious and more important smoked salmon group.

'Getting on all right, girls?' she asked us, and we murmured just fine, thanks.

'What'll we do?' Fleur asked in a whisper when she'd gone.

I shook my head. 'I'll pop over to the other sweet nibbles group and see if they've got anything to lend us,' I said.

They didn't have. Su had been given chocolate and coconut and Donna had raisins but they said they needed them all. It didn't matter much anyway, because by the time I'd wandered around to see what everyone else was doing and gone back to Fleur, she'd eaten nearly all the biscuit mixture out of the bowl.

'It was raw!' I said. 'How could you eat it just like that?'

'Easily,' she said. 'It's just like licking the bowl round only there's more of it. Besides, I was starving. All I've eaten today is two dry biscuits and a piece of cheese.'

'What'll we do?!' Cerise said in alarm.

'We'll just have to say our biscuits have disappeared in the ovens somewhere,' Fleur shrugged. 'It could easily happen with twenty or so girls and ten or more ovens. Miss Attlee won't even remember who's done what, I bet!'

'She will!' Cerise said, wide-eyed and frightend.

'Maybe we can just stand near the other sweet nibbles lot and just sort of pretend ours is in with theirs,' I said.

And then I got a brilliant idea. When we'd been discussing the Revue with our drama teacher, Mr Lloyd, he'd told us that we needed a backcloth of painted scenery and that he'd let us choose one from a selection that they had for school plays. He was free most last periods in the afternoon, if we wanted to go with him and look through what was available.

I clicked my fingers. 'Time to go and see Mr Lloyd!' I said to Fleur and Cerise. 'As MC I really feel I need to get the Revue backdrop fixed up as soon as possible. This afternoon, in fact.'

'And I need to help you. Second opinion and all that,' Fleur said quickly.

'Third opinion?' Cerise asked plaintively.

'Not sure about that,' I said. 'On the other hand if you are going to be on stage first, mind, maybe you need to see the backcloth.' I looked at Cerise thoughtfully, 'You said you didn't want to be first, though, didn't you?'

'I've changed my mind!' she said.

I went over to Miss Attlee, who was opening gallons of lemonade and pouring it into a cauldron thing. 'Could you possibly excuse us for a while?' I asked politely. 'I promised Mr Lloyd that we'd go over and see him about something important. For the charity shield, you know.'

'All of you?' Miss Attlee asked, and I nodded.

'Have you finished the things you were supposed to make?'

'Yes. *Completely* finished them,' I said truthfully. 'We've er . . . used all the ingredients and er . . . there's nothing else we can do.'

'So will you ask one of the other girls to get them out of the oven for you?'

I nodded, crossing my fingers.

'Well, mind that you report back before the end of the lesson, then,' she said, and the three of us disappeared like lightning.

Mr Lloyd showed us what he had, which wasn't much, and although Cerise was desperate to have the sugar-plum-fairy pink scene which had been the backcloth for *Sleeping Beauty*, in the end we chose a fairly ordinary sort of scene which had been used for *Romeo and Juliet* two years ago. It had a lot of houses on the right and a great flight of steps on the left and a couple of trees. It was pretty dull and uninteresting, really, but hopefully the audience would be so taken with what was going on on the stage that they'd hardly notice it.

We hung about as long as possible asking Mr Lloyd daft questions, then timed it so that we got back to the cookery rooms just before the last bell. When we quietly slipped in, all the class was standing about looking pleased with themselves and Miss Attlee was surveying a whole army of dainty bits and pieces cooling on wire trays in front of her.

Only Alison noticed our reappearance. She was standing beside some miniature sausage rolls baked so long so that they were hard, flat and dark brown.

'Where have you lot been?' she asked suspiciously, 'and where's the food you've made?'

'All over there!' Fleur said, airily waving a hand towards the wire trays.

'I didn't see you put any out,' she said. 'I reckon you've . . .'

'*They're* nice,' Fleur said, pointing to the sausage rolls. 'Dog biscuits, are they?'

Luckily, just as Alison took a threatening step towards Fleur, Miss Attlee started coming round on a tour of inspection. After pausing for a moment at the sausage rolls and looking at them curiously she moved on, nodding her approval.

'Very nice, girls,' she said, walking up and down looking at everything. 'I'm sure the governors will be most impressed at what you've achieved. Some of these things look absolutely delicious.' She moved slowly down past Annabel's golden vol-au-vents towards Su's coconut dreams. 'I did think I'd allowed for slightly more sweet things,' she said thoughtfully. 'I must have got my calculations wrong.'

She gave a merry laugh, 'I'm losing my touch – it must be my age!' she said, and Fleur, Cerise and I just nudged each other.

Chapter Ten

'THERE'S NO BUSINESS LIKE REVUE BUSINESS . . .'

'There's no business like Revue business . . .' I sang tunelessly at breakfast, careering round the kitchen with two carrier bags and picking up lists, pens, clipboards and bits and pieces of food to pack away and eat later.

It was Revue day and everyone in the first year who was involved – and that was most of us – was staying after school ready for curtain up (although there wasn't actually a curtain) at seven o'clock.

Mum looked up from her two slices of buttered toast. 'You sound happy, dear. Looking forward to tonight, are you?'

'Course,' I said.

There was a slight pause and she cleared her throat. 'I take it that you've enjoyed your first term, then, have you?'

'Maybe . . .' I said evasively.

'Now, come on – the truth. You've settled in really well!' She paused to lick a scrap of marmalade from her finger. 'Of course, you never tell me anything and I know you wouldn't actually *admit* that you liked it there . . .'

'Well,' I said again, and then grinned, 'it's not bad. I suppose I might go back again next term . . .'

I grabbed my duffle coat from the hall and had one final look round the kitchen. 'I hope I haven't forgotten anything,' I said and, picking up my carrier bags, I rattled them importantly. 'It's a really vital job, you know – MC.'

'I know!' Mum said. 'The most vital. Dad and I will be sitting in that audience tonight knowing it's all down to you.'

I smirked a bit.

'Break a leg, then!' she said as she saw me off.

I looked at her, shocked. 'That's not very nice.'

She laughed. 'That's what you say in the theatre instead of wishing anyone good luck. See you later!'

I sat down at the front of the school bus – most of the other first years were up at the back but there wasn't enough room for me. The minute the bus started Philippa, defying a roar from the driver, ran down the aisle and flung herself into the seat next to me.

'Guess what?!' she asked excitedly.

I rolled my eyes. 'I can't! Someone in the second year expecting triplets? Or . . .' I racked my brains for something even more ridiculous . . . 'a famous Hollywood producer is coming to the Revue?'

'No! Better!'

'A member of the royal family coming to present the charity shield?'

'Better!'

'What, then? And before you tell me I don't believe it!'

Her eyes gleamed. 'There's a new girl coming next term – a new girl who's a TV star!'

'Go on!'

'This time it's definitely and absolutely true . . . my mum knows the school secretary's sister and she told her that this girl is a proper TV star and in one of the soaps.'

'But someone like that would go to stage school,' I said witheringly. 'She'd go where they had special drama classes and singing lessons and everything.'

'Well, I'm only telling you what's been passed on to me in strictest confidence,' Philippa said. 'Apparently her parents have moved nearby and because she's getting a bit above herself, they want her to go to an ordinary school and mix with ordinary girls.'

'Oh well, we'll see, shall we?' I grinned, not believing a word. 'All ready for tonight?' I asked her.

'Oh yes!' she said. 'Mum's bought a new duvet cover for the spare room and we've put flowers in there and a blush pink lampshade and . . .'

'Oh, dear, oh, dear,' I said, shaking my head, 'not tonight: *Annabel coming to stay*, tonight: *the Revue!*'

'Oh yes!' she said. 'Annabel and I have been practising like mad and we're all ready. We've brought everything with us. Annabel's brought her overnight stuff too,' she couldn't resist adding, 'and she's got real silk pyjamas!'

Mrs Mackie was in a wonderfully jovial mood at register, even when Alice, best at maths so naturally treasurer of our charity shield project, announced that even with Fleur's slimming money and someone else's sponsored litter-pick-up money, we weren't going to win the shield. We'd already heard that the Fifth year, who'd all done a whole term of baby-sitting entirely for charity shield funds, had walked off with it hands down.

'It was a wonderful effort, though, girls,' Mrs Mackie said. 'Of course, the fifth year are of an age when they can be employed, so it's ludicrous to try and pit eleven-year-olds against those who can draw real wages. In the circumstances I think you've done remarkably well, and I'm really looking forward to seeing your performances tonight.'

Praise from Mrs Mackie was real praise, and everyone turned to beam at everyone else.

'I have a few changes to tell you about for next year,' she said after she'd taken the register. 'First of all – a change of classroom. You'll still be with me, of course, but owing to pressure of space we'll be moving into what was once the language block. The whole school is being reshuffled, so for a while it will be difficult to work out where everyone is.'

'Sit next to me if you can find the class?' Fleur asked in a whisper.

'Course!' I said.

'The other change is that next year we've got a new girl joining us,' Mrs Mackie went on.

Philippa wriggled in her seat and nudged or poked everyone close to her. 'You wait . . . I told you . . .' I heard her mutter.

'Now, I hope there's not going to be any silliness between you girls . . .' Mrs Mackie broke off and looked hard at Cerise here, 'when I tell you that this particular girl comes from a stage school and has already appeared in certain television programmes.'

'Told you!' Philippa said in a much louder and triumphant voice. 'Didn't I tell everyone! I said she was coming and no one believed me!'

'I haven't actually seen her on television myself,' Mrs Mackie said, 'but apparently she's occasionally in one of the soaps.' She looked down at a piece of paper, 'It's called *Village Life*, I believe.'

Cerise gave a short scream. '*Village Life!*

Patrick Parker's in that and he's gorgeous!'

'Thank you, Cerise,' Mrs. Mackie said. 'Now, I've told you all this so you can get over any initial excitement and just treat Jane as an ordinary pupil.' She looked at us over her glasses, 'You will, won't you?'

'I don't even like *Village Life*. I think it's stupid,' Alison said sourly, but Mrs Mackie went out of the classroom then and the rest of us spent several minutes excitedly trying to work out who Jane was, what part she played and whether we liked her or not.

'Patrick Parker . . .' Cerise said dreamily. 'D'you think this new girl will be able to get signed photographs of him?'

'Sure to,' Fleur said.

'If they're friendly enough he might even bring her to school sometimes,' I added casually.

Cerise gave a little scream. 'D'you really think so? I feel positively sick!'

'Excuse me!' Philippa said loudly. 'I think apologies are due, don't you? I told everyone she was coming, didn't I? I told everyone and no one believed me!'

The morning went on as usual but in the afternoon we didn't do much work at all. We had a final rehearsal to iron out any last-minute problems. Mr Lloyd and Mrs Mullins came along to help and then we went into the assembly hall to start putting the chairs out.

Mr Lloyd had got the backcloth up already

(I ticked off backcloth from my checklist), and he was also looking after the sound system for us (sound system √). I made sure the right tape was there, starting with cancan music (music √) and then went round to everyone and made sure they knew what order they were on and that they had all their bits and pieces with them (cast: accessories √). I was really a most efficient and meticulous MC, even down to hourly checks on Donna's white rabbit (bunny √).

She'd used a toy rabbit for rehearsals, but apparently when she was conjuring properly on stage she always used Woffles, a real live white rabbit. She said it appeared out of a concealed compartment at the bottom of a top hat to loud 'Aahs' from the audience. Apparently Su, magician's assistant, had been round to Donna's house a few times to rehearse with it and was now fully bunny-aware.

When all the chairs had been put out and we'd done absolutely everything we could think of, we laid all the props ready and in order and I walked up and down a lot, looking important but not doing much.

About five o'clock we settled down for a bit of a picnic backstage, all sitting on the floor except for Woffles who was in his cage and nibbling a carrot. Cerise was the only one who'd changed into her costume already and it was spread out in frills and flounces all round her, taking up enough room for four girls. Her mum had sent in some flowers at lunchtime and these were pinned in her hair already and going brown round the edges.

Picnic over, I went down the list of people who weren't actually on stage but had jobs to do, and made sure that they knew what they were doing. It had been suggested that Alison should be a bouncer to turn people away at the door who hadn't got tickets but, in the end, she'd been roped in by Alice to turn the pages of her sheet music. Nearly everyone had something to do; two girls we just couldn't think of a job for had, at the last minute, decided to dress up in their mums' best clothes and, pretending to be school governors, rush on stage during Erica's impersonations of teachers shouting, '*This is an outrage!*' Some girls were helping the audience to their seats, a couple were out in the car park directing traffic. We'd thought of absolutely everything.

Well, nearly everything; what we hadn't thought of was that someone might have an accident. It was when everyone was getting changed and pretending to each other that they were going to be too terrified to go on, and I was striding about waving my clipboard a lot.

'Help!' Donna called from backstage. 'It's Su! She's fallen down some steps!'

'Is she all right?' I said, first on the scene.

Su looked white and Donna looked worried.

'No. I think she's broken her leg!' Donna said.

Well, you can imagine what I thought: *Mum*! It was all her fault; she'd said break a leg, and now someone had.

Mrs Mullins, Mr Lloyd and everyone else rushed to help her and Mrs Mullins said she didn't think it was a break, but she'd have to take her to hospital for an X-ray just to make sure.

They went off and we all stood round looking at each other wondering what we ought to do.

'Don't just stand there!' Mr Lloyd said. 'The audience is starting to arrive!'

Everyone looked at me. 'We . . . we'll change the running order,' I said. 'We'll put Donna and Su last and hope that Su will be back from hospital by nine o'clock and be able to go on.'

'Not with a broken leg she won't,' Annabel said.

'Maybe it'll just be twisted and they'll bind it up so she can walk on it,' I said. 'If she doesn't arrive we'll think of something else.'

There was a scream from Cerise who was peering round at the audience. 'Mummy's here and she's bought my great big Pooh bear mascot with her. Look! He's sitting in the seat right next to her.'

'I hope he bought his own ticket,' Fleur said.

So . . . the show went on. I have to say it: Cerise was fantastic; everyone loved her cancan, she did two encores and during the second one her shoe flew off and landed in the lap of a governor, who didn't seem to mind a bit. Alice's violin solo was next, bringing, as Mrs Mackie said later, 'a touch of class to the proceedings', and then the others followed in quick succession.

It got to nine-fifteen and Sammy and Paula, last act, were on and doing their Victoria Wood number, but there was still no sign of Mrs Mullins or Su.

Donna rushed up, looking desperate. 'I can't go on on my own!' she said. 'I need someone to hand me all the things. I'll get into a terrible muddle otherwise.'

'I'll have to do it!' I said recklessly, 'just get me into Su's sequins!'

'D'you really think you should?' Fleur asked – she was backstage to help everyone get dressed and looking really slim. 'You know what you're like . . .'

'I don't know what you mean,' I said indignantly. 'All I've got to do is stand there and hand things to Donna. Anyone can do *that*, can't they?'

'Hmm. Maybe . . .' Fleur said.

I squeezed into the sequinned costume but there was no time to try and find a mirror to admire myself because we were on.

I gave mum and dad a quick wave – just so

they'd know it was me looking glamorous – and then turned my attention to Donna. I'd seen the act a few times so I knew what to do. I just had to stand there smiling and bowing and pointing at Donna as if she was doing something really clever.

She was quite good, actually. She did some card tricks, inviting a member of the audience – Mrs Mackie – to come and 'choose any card' and finding them again in a new pack. That went well except I didn't hold out the magic box that Donna had to drop the cards into quite quickly enough and they all fell on the floor. The audience laughed, though, so I think they thought it was deliberate.

They laughed again when I gave Donna the wrong empty cannister in which hundreds of silk scarves were supposed to appear, because it really *was* empty. I found the scarves a minute later when I picked up another 'completely empty canister' and they fell out of the bottom and landed in a tangled heap at Donna's feet.

Next came the amazing disappearing magic wand, which didn't disappear for long because it dropped out of my sleeve and fell to the floor with a clatter, then I turned too quickly and nearly knocked down the table – the audience really roared at that.

Donna was looking annoyed by now so I thought I'd try really really hard and get her grand finale: *Woffles the Amazing Disappearing Rabbit*, absolutely right.

I showed the audience the completely empty top hat and then handed it to Donna with a flourish.

'Now, I'm going to wave my magic wand over this completely empty hat . . .' she said to the audience, 'and then I will hand it back to my assistant!'

She turned slightly away from the audience. 'Put the hat down flat on the table,' she whispered to me, 'then put your hand in and push the bottom until the rabbit appears.'

'Right!' I said in an undertone.

I put it flat on the table and, while Donna did all sorts of magical flourishes above the hat, pushed at the false bottom. I held my breath; the bottom had moved and I could feel fur – but bunny wasn't moving. I poked at him gently; he was supposed to poke his head out of the hat and look cute and then Donna was going to pick him up.

I gave Donna a sickly smile and stirred bunny around a bit with my finger, but he still wouldn't move.

Donna's magical flourishes were becoming a bit desperate, the audience was tittering.

'What're you doing?' she hissed. 'Haven't you got to him?'

'I have but he won't move!' I hissed back.

'What?!'

'He won't budge.' I looked at her mournfully. 'I think I've killed him. I must have been poking too hard.'

'For goodness' sake . . .' she began.

'It's okay,' I said,'leave it to me.' As MC I owed it to Donna and the Revue to save the day; I'd admit to the audience that it was all my fault; I'd take the blame completely.

I bravely turned to face the audience. 'I'm very sorry,' I said, 'but I'm afraid that we won't be able to go on with this trick because I've killed the rabbit . . .'

The audience howled with laughter and I looked at them in surprise. How mean could you get?

'Don't be stupid!' Donna said, breaking in crossly. 'I told you before we went on that I was going back to the toy rabbit because it was only Su who knew how to handle the real one!'

'You didn't!' I said.

'I did! You were too busy admiring yourself in those sequins to take any notice, though.'

While the audience rolled about on the floor laughing, Donna managed to get the toy rabbit out of the hat and finish her act, then we cleared the stage and everyone went back on to take a final bow. Or three, actually.

Mrs Mackie came backstage straight away. 'Wonderful!' she said. 'And what a clever idea to make all the magic tricks go wrong – and the dead bunny and the pretend – row on stage were just great. They made a marvellous finish!'

'Glad you liked them,' I muttered.

'I've just seen Miss Harmer and she was most impressed,' Mrs Mackie went on. 'Although you haven't won the charity shield she's having a new little cup engraved for you – for the most original and entertaining charity shield project.'

'Great!' we said, and then we all had three cheers for the charity shield and three for Mrs Mackie and then three more for the rest of us.

Taking everything into consideration, I'd quite enjoyed my first term . . .

Read more about Mickey, Cerise, Fleur and the other first year girls at Park Wood Girls' School in:

School Friends 2: *The Star*

Mrs Mackie didn't know what to make of Araminta Eversage, and Fleur and I thought she sounded more like a herb shampoo than a girl. She'd come from drama school though, and was already, according to her, star of stage, screen and catfood advertisements. She created havoc: Philippa was torn between her and Annabel, Cerise became ten times as silly and Mrs Mackie and Miss Harmer nearly came to blows. And then the camera team came to school . . .

Also by Mary Hooper

CASSIE

Cassie's one wish is to be a journalist, in a trench coat, carrying a reporter's note book, hot on the trail . . .

So when she gets a job as a Junior on the Weekly Echo her dream comes true. Or does it? Making endless cups of coffee, columns of supermarket bargains. Not *another* hundredth birthday!

But then there's always Gavin, the dashing photographer from *Sixteen-On*, or Simon, who's never far from Cassie's side.

Mary Hooper

LEXIE

Subtract one house-trained Mum; add one undomesticated Dad and divide by two unsuspecting daughters – the result? Disaster!

Lexie soon discovers that life with Dad is going to test her powers of endurance to the limits. If he's not chasing away the gorgeous, unattainable Laurie Clark, he's busy flooding the kitchen or covering the living room with wall-to-wall fluff. And if she so much as sets eyes on another take-away pizza . . .